Praise for *The Long Afternoon:*

'Lovingly recreates the glamour of the jazz age and the beauty of the French Riviera in the shadow of World War II'

Publishing News

'Place and time are vividly evoked ... real descriptive power'

The Lady

'Waterfield is good at re-creating the ease and the idleness of their existence, cushioned by faithful servants and almost excluding the French. He communicates its attractiveness while gently exposing its self-indulgence ... Waterfield's light touch makes it easy to read'

TLS

'Waterfield evokes their hypochondriac rituals with sympathy and with an irony that is intensified when their two sons, educated in England and hardly acquainted with their parents, visit in the late 1930s. But the Williamsons' fragile existence is disintegrating, and when they are finally destroyed by the Second World War, the couple achieves ... genuine pathos'

Sunday Times

'... Vibrant. Henry and Helen Williamson leave England to live on the French Riviera. However their blind belief that the international upheaval of events leading up to the Second World War cannot disrupt their tennis club and tea-room existence is sadly misplaced'

Bookseller

⊰⊱ Giles Waterfield ⊰⊱

THE LONG AFTERNOON

review

First published in Great Britain in 2000
by REVIEW

An imprint of Headline Book Publishing

First published in paperback in 2001

10 9 8 7

ISBN 0 7472 6848 7

Typeset by Letterpart Ltd
Reigate, Surrey

Printed and bound in Great Britain by
Clays Ltd, St Ives plc.

Headline Book Publishing
A division of Hodder Headline
338 Euston Road
London NW1 3BH

www.headline.co.uk
www.hodderheadline.com

For my brother

❖⟶ ACKNOWLEDGEMENTS ⟶❖

For their encouragement and good advice, I would like to thank Rupert Christiansen, Charlotte Gere, Lucy Hughes Hallett, Sarah Lutyens, Hazel Orme, Felicity Rubinstein, Paul Ryan, Nancy Tennant and William Waterfield. At Review, I am very grateful for their sympathetic professionalism to Ros Ellis, David Grogan, Mary-Anne Harrington, Peter Ward and above all Geraldine Cooke.

Up to 1860 it was a picturesque fishing town, with a few scattered villas let to strangers in the neighbouring groves, and all its surroundings were most beautiful and attractive; now much of its two lovely bays is filled with hideous and stuccoed villas in the worst taste. The curious old walls are destroyed, and pretentious paved promenades have taken the place of the beautiful walks under tamarisk groves by the sea shore. Artistically, Mentone is vulgarised and ruined, but its dry sunny climate is delicious, its flowers exquisite, and its excursions – for good walkers – are inexhaustible and full of intcrest.

AUGUSTUS HARE, *South-Eastern France*, 1890

Everything in this favoured locality is suited to the requirements of invalids and persons of delicate constitution. The climate is, perhaps, the mildest upon the entire coast. Nowhere on the northern Mediterranean shore does the lemon tree grow with equal luxuriance. Fogs and dews are unknown, the sky is cloudless. The town is so encircled by mountains that the mistral is scarcely even felt, and the temperature scarcely ever falls below the freezing point. Persons affected with pulmonary disease, either in the first or second stages, derive great benefit from passing the winter there.

Mentone strikes the stranger as a somewhat dull place. An air of languid repose pervades it; there is no keen edge to its breeze, no crisp freshness in the breath of its sea. Whether it is owing to the shadow of its lofty mountains brooding over its narrow strip of ground, or to the presence in its streets, when the sun shines, of so many faces on which the seal of death is set, certainly a kind of gloom pervades it, which is somewhat depressing. A well-known writer, whose own fate was to die and be buried there, called it 'that stuffy morgue, Menton'.

THOMAS COOK AND SON, *The Travellers' Handbook for the Riviera (Marseilles to Leghorn) and the Pyrenees (Biarritz to Marseilles)*, 1912

Y ES, SHE DID LIKE THE HOUSE. 'Built of stone' the agent M. Achille Isnard of Mentone announced on behalf of the auctioneers, Messrs Hampton of Cockspur Street, London SW, 're-modelled by the present owner only a few years back, entirely regardless of cost, the whole being complete in every minute detail ...' In the words of the charmingly attentive young agent who was so polite over understanding her not very fluent French, it was *'fort bien située'*. It commanded a fine prospect of the sea and the Old Town, enjoying, as the particulars put it, 'a magnificent and high position in one of the loveliest spots of this enchanting district'. Even though the distance from garden to shore was at least two hundred yards – or metres, as she supposed she must learn to call them, and certainly she could not think of the French word for 'yard' – from the highest terrace one felt the sea lay at the garden's edge. The water was absurdly blue, so that when she died twenty-eight years later her last memory, in the strange, sudden ebbing of strength that announced the final moment she had constantly dreaded, was of the shining Mediterranean that shimmered beneath her. The Mediterranean, its very name filled with associations (though Henry knew his classical associations better than she did), seemed to smile at her, promising ease and happiness. Perhaps the house itself will bring ease and happiness, she thought.

The house, she supposed, was quite ordinary, even if 'of a Very Imposing Character in the Italian Style', in the manner of many villas erected, in the past twenty years, all over the olive groves and the soft wildness of the coast beside the ancient republic of Mentone. No doubt Mr Hare (whose entertaining book on southern France she had been reading in the hotel) was right to condemn such houses in the vigorous way he did. But was it so improper to be attracted by a building with yellow ochre walls and a verandah laden with what must be wisteria along the entrance front and a handsome first-floor balcony and on all three floors double windows with great green shutters (*persiennes*, they were called — was it really the Persians who had invented these useful things?). She supposed it was wrong of the builder to have altered an old farmhouse in order to erect this modern house, but she was not convinced.

The agent, smiling sweetly by this time, told her that the vaulted ceiling in the entrance hall belonged to an old building that had provided the core of the new house twenty years earlier. But must she despise it because Mr Hare didn't like houses of the sort? She would have appealed to Henry for his views had he been there — she really could not imagine where he was — she would have asked him whether she was permitted to like the house aesthetically, so to speak, as well as for its position and convenience. And if they did not buy this house, on grounds of principle, what would they buy? If they chose something older in the town itself, rather than in what she supposed was a Mediterranean suburb — detestable word — then someone else would buy it and probably would not appreciate the quality of the garden which, goodness knows, she did, and she noticed an olive tree that stood conveniently beside her. She looked admiringly at it, laid one hand on it and moved naturally, she thought, into a poetic pose, half leaning, half standing, like a classical nymph on Mount Olympus. She found herself impelled to gaze, with what she felt was a soulful look, at the ocean beneath. As she did so, she remembered that the agent was standing beside her. She turned towards him. He, too, was staring into the distance.

'*Ravissante*,' she said, turning her neck with an eloquent sketchy airiness, since most of her limbs were still engaged in the leaning pose. *Ravissante* was a good sort of word, applicable to almost anything, though not perhaps everything male. A moment later, '*Enfin, il vous plaît, le jardin, Madame?*' he enquired, again with a freshness and charm one did not associate with the French. But she supposed that here in Mentone they were a long way from Paris and close to Italy, and people had a chance to develop in a more natural way. Yes, it did please her, the garden, she replied, even though the agent's particulars made it sound so dull, and did not evoke the magic of the situation, half-way between mountain and sea:

THE GROUNDS — *Palm Trees affording cool and fragrant retreat* — *Pretty Grotto, Rock Garden, Lily Pond* — *Numerous shrubs and Tropical Plants* — *Valuable Succulent Garden containing a choice selection of Rare Plants* — *Heliotrope and Carnation Borders* — *Stone-built Motor Garage* . . .

How could the garden not please, created as it was on six long-established terraces climbing the hill, with only the palm trees and the early mimosa — the inexpressibly soft yet gaudy, playful and high-scented mimosa, preening itself against the sky — to indicate that this was not the natural countryside of the Riviera?

'*C'est ravissant*,' she was about to say again and recalled that the word was suggestive as well as slightly monotonous, so she plumped for '*merveilleux*' instead. She hoped he thought her French was quite good, and he should certainly be pleased that she was taking the trouble to speak it when so many English people on the Riviera never tried at all. Do the French use superlatives as we do? she wondered fleetingly.

The young man seemed pleased and asked hopefully whether she liked Menton. Yes, she affirmed, which was the right thing to say since he had been born in the town and had always lived here, though he hoped one day to go to London which he had heard was *formidable*. It was *formidable*, she assured him ironically, shuddering at the thought of that harsh and dirty place, seat of imperial authority. At his suggestion they walked up the steps to the verandah and entered the house.

'*Alors qu'est-ce que c'est que Madame voudrait voir?*' asked the attentive young man, whose name she could not remember, though of course that was easier in France where one was not obliged to use the individual name. Oh, everything, she wanted to see everything, even the coal-hole. After all, she reminded herself, allowing herself a smile because she spoke about her origins so little — partly because people seldom enquired although they must wonder where the money came from — she was the daughter of a manufacturer of collar studs, who had spent the whole of his professional life until he was seventy-one creating and controlling a manufactury in Derby. She must not forget that she was her father's daughter, tempting though it might be to do so. Papa would have looked at every detail of a house he was buying. Indeed, she remembered him doing so in Staffordshire, and though she was not sure that she herself would be able to understand things like the heating system, she would do what she could. So yes, everything, she told him – and certainly all the servants' accommodation since she could not live in a house where the servants had bad rooms.

This seemed to surprise him, though he did not say so, merely opening his eyes quite wide and looking at her as though she were an unusual person. He might think, perhaps, that she was very compassionate or then again he might think that she was foolish. So since he seemed such a nice young man she explained. 'I was brought up,' she said, 'to think that one's servants, though called to a position of service, are people just as good as oneself in the sight of God, and that if they live in one's house they become part of one's family. In spite of the difference in fortune and position, one must be sure that they are happy and agree among themselves' (though goodness knows that is some-times hard to achieve, she thought, people seemed naturally designed to bicker, women especially) 'and that they have pleasant rooms and comforts and proper light and air.' And she reflected that she could not bear frowning faces around her and was immediately anxious if one of her servants seemed cold or unfriendly. She had to know what disturbed them, if they would only tell her. Sometimes, asserting their privacy, they would not.

She continued to ruminate, all the while admiring, with a growing feeling that this was the house where she would live, the vault of the hall with its cast-iron lamp in the centre and the carved wooden fireplace, the room cool and reflective after the brilliance of the garden.

It was vital they should choose the right house, a house which would become their home, and where they would spend so many years. She liked to think that it was the place where they would enjoy the afternoon of their lives. She hoped it would be a long afternoon, and would melt only gradually into the evening, and then the night.

('Lounge Entrance Hall,' announced the brochure, 'with vaulted ceiling and very handsome wrought iron and plate glass door, 19ft. by 14 ft. paved with mosaic, lighted by two windows with leaded diamond panes, having deep marble sills, and opening by French casement windows on to the Verandah with the Corinthian columns which give a point of decoration and ornamentation to the exterior.')

'*Et voici le salon,*' said the agent. The room was very large, just the place for big parties or for entertaining the cream of Mentone society, whatever that might consist of. It had two fireplaces, one with a mirror over it, and two French windows (what were they called in French?) on to the verandah, and a bow window with a view of the garden. With no furniture in it, the room was almost daunting. She asked him who had lived in the house before. An English lady, he said, Madame Groves, who had lived quite quietly but liked a good deal of space and had a nephew who stayed very often. She had never heard of a Mrs Groves with money, but how intriguing, she thought. What could that nephew have been doing? Was he fortune-hunting? Was he really her nephew?

The dining room, on the other side of the hall from the drawing room, interrupted these thoughts. It, too, looked on to the verandah and, though slightly dark, was perfectly dignified, furnished by the 'massive carved walnutwood mantelpiece' in Smoking Room Baroque. The kitchen, large and cheerful with red octagonal tiles, and the little servants' hall (he called it '*l'office*') and the back door, with more wisteria growing over it, were all that could be desired. She climbed with enthusiasm up the steep stairs that led to the servants' bedrooms above the kitchen, with their own bright view of the town. 'Oh, I could live in these little rooms,' she cried to the young man.

'*Mais ça ne sera pas nécessaire,*' he answered seriously. '*Je pense que le premier étage plaira à Madame.*'

He was right. How could she not be pleased by these high rooms, all facing the sea, the square bedroom in the corner above the dining room, the little dressing room, the central room above the hall? This was like the apartment of a prince, she thought. She tried to forget that it was not unlike the house she and Henry had had during their last dismal posting, in Delhi, those cruel weeks when her child was taken from her, when the foul vicious climate of that detestable country destroyed her precious daughter. She suppressed these unendurable thoughts but shuddered a little. Then they walked up a few stairs and the young man said, '*Le petit salon,*' as though he expected her to know what this room would be, opened a door and made way for her to go in, looking at her expectantly the while. And then she knew without any doubt at all that this was the ideal house for Henry and herself and the boys, though they had seen so few and could hardly make comparisons, and that she must buy it or, rather, they must. And she knew that Henry (where was Henry, why was he not here, what could he be doing in the town at such an important moment?) would like it too.

She had been standing at the threshold all this while, her hand on the door frame, gazing into the room, her eyes led by the light on to the balcony. Here she could be happy, she knew, here she could become the assured person, the erudite and accomplished talker, the hostess, the mother, the wife, she had always wanted to be. If only India had not wounded her so severely. Behind her the agent shifted slightly. She must go in.

The room was empty and dark by contrast with the clear spring sunshine. Her gaze was dominated by the view out of the two windows to the sea. The windows drew her towards the light, so that the drawing room and the balcony became one large yet human and contained space, made for conversation among people at ease with one another. The room itself — what had he called it: the *petit salon*? — bare as it was, with the marks of furniture against the walls, already seemed sociable with its striped green wallpaper and the glass over the chimneypiece. Her furniture, she knew at once, would feel at home here. The portrait of her father (no matching portrait of her mother, of course) would hang on the right. Her own portrait would go opposite the fireplace — though perhaps Henry had been right in suggesting that a full length was too large for most rooms. Would her image, in a long white dress, idyllic in a landscape setting, gazing with gentle reverie at a bush, overpower the room? What a shame that they had no portrait of Henry, so absurd of him to claim there was no reason to paint him, that he was a person of no importance, since portraiture should commemorate personality and not position. And in any case he was very distinguished. They moved towards the balcony and the young man, Monsieur Étienne she thought he was called, bent down to open the window. And there was the perfect balcony, the balcony of balconies, five-sided, with a balustrade: here she could survey the garden, the cypresses towering above, the Old Town of Mentone, the new villas and hotels stretching along the promenade de Garavan towards the memorial to Queen Victoria. Smiling at the pleasure she displayed, the young man gestured like an artist revealing a painting towards the view behind them. She turned to admire the slope of the hill, with its old cultivated terraces interrupted here and there by the solid exuberance of villas like this one. Behind the slopes, massive, grey, yet not menacing, rose the immense boulder of the mountain. She looked at Monsieur Étienne, enquiringly, and he said, '*Le Berceau, Madame, plus que mille mètres de hauteur.*' She smiled at him, thankful that she would never have to attempt its height for herself.

As they contemplated the view, they heard a noise outside. It was a carriage, drawn by two horses (how very extravagant of him to take a two-horse carriage, she thought fondly). It moved cautiously as though the driver were unfamiliar with the route, up the drive and on to the circular sweep of gravel with its palm trees and mimosa in front of the house. The carriage stopped, waveringly, before the front door and from it, calm, tall, a little pink in the sun, self-deprecating, kind, perfect, stepped Henry. Oh he was perfect, how fortunate she was, and as she leant from the balcony to call his name she saw him look up, as anyone would, faced by so beautiful a balcony. He glimpsed her through the leaves and waved. It was a moment of happiness, pure unclouded emotion, she would reflect in later days, when somehow joy seemed always to be vitiated by anxieties and illness. He smiled so sweetly, with such affection, and waved at her and left the carriage and called to her, 'Jolly nice place, darling!' It was easy from that balcony to communicate with someone below, however far they might seem. She called back, 'Darling, I think it's lovely,' and then, remembering the agent who though he said he did not speak English certainly must understand it, added, 'I mean there are problems but it is very pleasant,' and felt absurd for having used such a limiting English word. Not just pleasant but exquisite, sheltered, pure . . . She told him to come upstairs, and Monsieur Étienne obligingly said he would find Monsieur and bring him up to the balcony. And when Henry arrived, quizzical, solicitous, sensitive, she did not ask him why he was so late and whether he had been feeling unwell but 'Darling, I think it's right,' she said, 'darling, I think it's ideal. I'm sure we'd be very happy here — don't you think so?' When he remarked that he had only just arrived and had hardly seen anything, she hurried on, 'You haven't seen it all but you will see it, you will, every room of it. Monsieur Étienne is so kind, and he will show us everything.'

They saw the rest of the house together. First of all the other rooms on the first floor. The side bedroom, looking out towards the Italian border, had a pretty painted ceiling, with garlands of flowers forming a canopy around the edges of the ceiling and an illusionistic sky with fluffy blue clouds. 'Now who did these?' he asked Monsieur Étienne, always anxious as he was to obtain facts about buildings and paintings, so sweet and curious of him, she thought. Monsieur Étienne replied that the ceiling paintings were a speciality of Mentone, and that the best were done, he thought, by a family called Cerruti, and he was confident that this family must have painted the ceilings in such an important house as Lou Paradou. 'Our bedroom?' he said, looking at the ceiling, and then 'I mean, your bedroom?'

She knew that the house contained more impressive rooms than this one and said, 'No, there is a whole other floor we must see.'

So they walked upstairs, with the agent in front, now more deferential and silent with the arrival of this English gentleman, so imposing, so correct even though he often smiled. She followed him eagerly but all the while looked back at Henry to see that he was content, while Henry moved more deliberately up the stairs, admiring the painted sky that adorned this ceiling too, and the view of the mountain from the staircase window.

On the upper floor the rooms rose high above the garden so that only the tops of the palm trees could be seen from the windows. From the summit of the tower, which gave the house a picturesquely irregular skyline, the windows looked over the bay and the Old Town. Would this room be ours, she wondered, or a guest room, or even Charles's, perhaps, when he was older since he would not be happy here now at his age? On the main front of the house were three principal rooms. 'Oh, it's perfect,' she said, 'so well planned and organised. This must be the guest room because we shall have lots of guests, I suppose, and this must be our bedroom, I think it belonged to Mrs ... the woman who was here before ... with its little *cabinet de toilette*, and this surely will be your room or will it be the schoolroom but perhaps it's too nice to be a schoolroom and if I were next door and trying to rest it would be disturbing to have the children there so probably your room, your dressing room, I mean,' she said, 'where you will do your work and write your books, my darling, though will it be big enough for all these purposes? But the important thing is that you should have your own den, now that you don't have your own office, which you miss.'

To which he replied, 'But I don't miss my office, either the room or the position, so that is no problem at all.'

They stopped talking and looked around them, at the room and the view and one another, aware in the softly bustling silence, which came upon the town at noon, that they might be about to settle one of the most important decisions of their lives. They had made so many decisions recently, Helen thought. The most important had been that Henry should leave the Indian Civil Service. He had resigned when he was just thirty and set, as his colleagues thought, upon a brilliant career. He had taken a first-class degree at Oxford and had passed first of his year into the Indian Civil Service — which, as everybody knew, took the best people, better than the Home Civil Service. There had been so many possibilities open to him but, alas, the Indian Civil Service, however glorious it might be, and part of the nation's duty, meant sacrifice not just of oneself but of one's family, sacrifice that might amount to death. Of course, his decision to resign had hardly been disputed since a man in his delicate health and desperately prone to asthma could not continue a career that endangered him and exposed his body, his poor weak lungs, to the horrors of the Indian climate, that cruel sun, that pitiless child-killing and man-killing heat. But it had not been easy. Not everyone had been understanding, and it had even been hinted that she had made him resign because she did not like India herself. There were only faint hints, mostly from the wives of his colleagues, probably annoyed that they could not have afforded to escape India themselves, but it was cruelly uncompassionate of people even to suggest such a thing. She found herself frowning and hastily suppressed this unattractive expression.

Then there was the decision about where to go, the attempt they had made to live in Staffordshire where she had grown up, and though she loved the house, which was very pretty and probably designed by Adams, her aunt was still living there and the climate in the Midlands, while hardly resembling India, was not suited to two people so delicate as themselves. They had moved instead to Cornwall, which had been very pleasant and they had enjoyed the house at Marazion, with its views of the sea and the unending cream and the delicious quietness, but it had still been too cool and damp there in winter, and the society, it had to be said, was very limited.

So finally they had decided to abandon England and look for a house in the South of France or possibly on the Italian Riviera (though it was rather less fashionable and one could not be altogether unaware of these things) where they could spend the greater part of the year. Many people, especially doctors, had spoken of Mentone as the warmest, most sheltered place in civilised Europe, the only possible place reasonably close to England for people with bad chests or prone to asthma. For a moment, now and then, she had wondered if this move was quite what Henry wanted, since, he had murmured once or twice, he had hoped to carry out some official work if he stayed in England. But she understood the medical truth, sad as it might be, and told him that such a decision might be fatal. She realised that, clever though he was, he was not always very practical and it was her duty to persuade him that practical decisions needed to be made.

When, a few days before, they had arrived in Mentone, so seductive, so easy, filled with orange trees and lemon trees, the town seeming to laugh with pleasure around its bay, all these difficult decisions became a great deal easier.

The young agent watched these charming but quiet people: she so pretty, so warm, so conscious of herself, clutched by some emotion which could not be divined but which must be associated with the house, he so kind and solicitous and so hard to understand. Sensing the recollections and hopes and anxieties that fluttered within them, he moved unobtrusively, muttering some apology, out of the room and into the passage. There he stood, not precisely eavesdropping but near at hand if needed.

'It's very beautiful,' Henry said, 'and very well planned. And the position . . . But to decide to live here when we have seen so few houses . . . Do you think you would be happy here, my dearest?'

'Yes, I do think so, I truly like it,' she said. 'Not only is it beautiful, but it's so sheltered and I'm sure it will always be warm here and it has exactly the space we needed, even if we had more children, which is not very likely.' (She spoke breathlessly here, and looked down at the floor.) 'And it's perfect for entertaining and for the servants. But do you like it, lovey darling? That's the most important thing.'

'Oh, yes, I like it, I think it's AI. And can we afford it?' he wondered, a little arch for a moment as was his custom when they talked about money, or at least about money on any scale. Yes, she replied, she had looked at the details and they could indeed afford it.

They summoned back Monsieur Étienne, who seemed astounded and delighted that in principle they had decided with such speed, and told them that it was one of the most beautiful houses in the town and that he was sure they would be happy there. Tactfully he gave them the house key and said they could stay as long as they liked but should deliver the key back before six o'clock, unless they would like him to collect it. He shook their hands warmly (such a strange habit, she thought, and not very healthy with all the germs around especially in France and, well scrubbed though he looked, she would have to wash her hands thoroughly, it was not his fault if he were the carrier of something, the most innocent people might be that). Then he went.

Still in the room that might be Henry's study or possibly the schoolroom, they looked at one another in the golden silence. She noticed the walls with their patterned wallpaper showing the marks where the previous owner's furniture had stood, and found herself busily wondering whether they would carpet the floors. Then she looked at him. He was staring at her, as she thought, with that strange look of his that combined diffidence with some other emotion — what was it? Could it be passion, and what was passion like? She had seen this look before on him but not for some time. Did he love her? she asked herself yet again. Was she forcing him to accept a way of life he did not like? And as she looked at him and was about to speak, he answered her question, not in words but by coming towards her and taking her hand and kissing her. Then he drew back his face and looked into her eyes and planted his lips fully upon hers. Then, 'Is the house what you want?' he said, and before she could reply or even know what he meant he kissed her again. 'Let us see the house,' he cried. 'Show me your house, Mrs Williamson, show me your new and beautiful house.' Catching her outstretched hand so that their two arms extended as one, he pulled her into the great empty space of the room and said more softly, 'Show me the house.'

The silence became deeper and the sun, now fully in the south, beat more strongly so that she was glad as they passed through the rooms, hand in hand, he leading her, she leaning a little against him from time to time, that the shutters were mostly closed and the rooms obscured. Now and again he would pause and look at her enquiringly and say such things as 'The children's room?' and then they would pass into another softly glowing space. It was quite straightforward to work out the future function of each room, though he did say, teasingly, 'Are there enough servants' rooms for the huge household which I am sure you plan?' Finally they came to the drawing room downstairs and there, swept away by affection and happiness, he took her in his arms and kissed her as he had not kissed her for many months and whispered in her ear that he loved her, and though she worried that other buyers might arrive and be amazed by the effect that the house had had on them, or that the gardener might appear, or the cab-driver might still be outside . . .

The largest contingent of invalids suffering from any one disease which reaches the Riviera is certainly the phthisical. By phthisis I mean a more or less progressive invasion of the air-cells of the lungs by proliferated endothelial cells (desquamative pneumonica, of Buhl) beginning usually at one apex and extending downwards. The 'consolidation' thus produced tends through obliteration of nutritive blood-vessels, as well as by the pressure of the new cells on the surrounding tissues, to sloughing and ulceration, and so to the formation of cavities. The disease may remain localised in one lung, or it may also attack the apex of the other, and large portions of both lungs may rapidly become involved. In other very chronic cases a connective-tissue growth developed in the interalveolar lung tissue, and fibrous bands or septa traverse the diseased parts of the lung. ... The great thing, it seems to me, is to get rid of the expression 'tuberculosis' as applied to chronic phthisis ...

As to the number of winters which patients who begin to benefit from the climate should spend on the Riviera it is impossible to speak with certainty, but putting aside expense and looking at the matter merely from an abstract point of view, I doubt whether at least three winters should not be reckoned on ...

EDWARD SPARKS, *The Riviera – Sketches of the Health Resorts of the North Mediterranean Coast of France and Italy from Hyères to Spezia*, 1879

⇥ JANUARY 1914 ⇤

'WHAT DO YOU THINK, AUNT SUSAN?'
Helen enquired. It was a question she had often
asked as a child of her imposing, clever, good-looking and
humorous aunt. With no mother of whom to ask questions, and a father who was seldom to be seen and seemed
little interested in her, Aunt Susan had become her guardian
and mentor. And since she acted also as governess, her aunt
shaped Helen's upbringing. There were not many friends of
her own age in Staffordshire. Nobody could be troubled to
find them: the landed families were too self-contained, and
her father did not seek association with trade or the
professions, and especially not medicine. Nor was her
horrid boarding-school, which she had pined to leave from
the moment she arrived there, any consolation: when she
left she wanted to see nobody there again. Until she met
Henry in the summer of 1901 and spent those idyllic
weeks with him at Blithbury, she was almost friendless.

It had been kind of her aunt to travel out with Miss
Gordon, the young woman recommended by the best possible sources as a governess, whom Helen had already seen in
London. They had arrived the day before, evidently having
made friends. Miss Gordon seemed at home already – she
was so natural, so calm, so well-mannered, so everything that
was best about Scotland (not that Helen knew clearly what

that meant, never having been there, but it seemed to apply). They were offering a handsome salary and the chance to go back to Scotland to see her family every summer, so she should be pleased. It appeared she was, since she had already expressed her delight in the garden, gazing at it as though absorbing its essence. And at dinner the night before, which Helen had rather dreaded, since she supposed they would be obliged to lunch and dine with the governess every day, Miss Gordon had answered perfectly all the questions they put to her about her past life and education.

'I consider you have made a very good decision, Helen,' said her aunt. 'She is a delightful girl. You would not have wanted a French governess, after all, with the children growing up chattering in French and playing with hoops in the public park or whatever French children do. Miss Gordon seems to me ideal.'

'Yes,' replied Helen. 'I hope she will be happy here, that is if she accepts the position. I wonder,' she continued musingly, 'if she has a young man at home.'

'No mention of one during our journey,' said her aunt. 'I am sure she can manage very well without. Living here, the danger is more likely to be an old man, captivated by her excellent qualities. But I hardly think you need worry about that just yet.'

'And do you think the children like her?'

'For the moment that's beside the point. They will learn to like her,' Aunt Susan pronounced. Her firmness touched her niece with a familiar sense of alarm. 'She will be a great addition to the household, and bring to the children's upbringing an element of discipline which you, my dear, and even Henry, sometimes forget.'

Helen pinched her lips together to prevent herself from pouting, or worse, as they sat among the tea things. '*Le five o'clock*' was an institution the Williamsons had not abandoned on coming to France. They were surprised to find how solid an institution afternoon tea appeared to be in the hotels and refreshment rooms of Mentone, and Aunt Susan had noticed a paragraph in the *Menton and Monte Carlo News*, which remarked that 'nowhere is afternoon tea more the fashion than at Nice'. It seemed to Aunt Susan pretty tame: even Staffordshire could offer brisker entertainment. But tea seemed to suit her niece. Helen still considered that a sandwich or two, cut very thin, and a small slice or two of cake, were indispensable for keeping up one's strength. She stared hard at the new Royal Worcester tea service from the Army and Navy Stores, chosen by her, which had arrived only the week before and was considered a great success. By concentrating on it she hoped to avert and even dispel the panic such words aroused in her. No, she could manage a house, and she could bring up children – and she spent much more time with them than many mothers did. She was not to be denied these achievements, just because Aunt Susan implied that she was an indulgent mother, and Henry an indulgent father. Her aunt, after all, had nothing to do, stuck in that big house in Staffordshire with nobody to talk to except her brother and the ducks, though they did say that she had come to be very much in demand with local society ...

'When do Charles and Francis come in to see you?' asked Aunt Susan. 'Charles is such a handsome little boy, and so intelligent, and very forward for five. But I suppose he has not had the chance of any education without a governess, out here in France.' Aunt Susan was of the school which believed that England, and by extension Britain, was the best country in the world and that other nations were only blessed when they imitated the source of all virtue. This, the French could hardly be said to do, though they seemed to have been trying harder lately to be a little more British.

Helen, suppressing once again a tremor of resentment, said she had done her best, and that Charles was already beginning to read on his own. It was not altogether true that she had done her best, since her elder son filled her with anxiety. He reminded her of her first child, Phoebe, who would have been so close to him in age; it was not altogether pleasant to remember. And he was an unusual boy, prone to putting penetrating questions of a sort one did not always want to hear. A moment later the nursemaid appeared. In her arms she carried Francis, aged two, but he wriggled free and ran to his mother. She embraced him eagerly. Within a moment he was absorbed in a pile of bricks extracted from a large wooden box, busy constructing castles and bridges.

Charles followed, more soberly. He was wearing a sailor suit and his hair was brushed down. He held a woolly bear, and smiled at the ladies. He walked to Aunt Susan and stood on his toes to kiss her. And then, as though recalling his manners, Helen thought, he crossed the room to his mother and kissed her too.

'Would you like me to read aloud to you?' Helen asked. 'Or perhaps you will ask Aunt Susan whether she would read to you. She reads very well. She read aloud to me every night when I was a child.'

Charles looked at his mother in that probing way he had, which preceded his awkward questions.

'Why did Aunt Susan read to you, Mamma?' he asked. 'Didn't you have a mamma of your own?'

No, she had had no mamma of her own. She remembered, or thought she remembered, a woman with long red hair on whose knee she would bounce up and down beside the fire. And she was almost sure she could see in her mind an evening when this woman, dressed in a big coat and hat, ran into her nursery and seized her and hugged her and stared into her eyes and said, 'Goodbye, my darling,' and then something she did not understand, choking rather in a way she did not associate with grown-ups. After that she never saw the woman again, and a day or two later Aunt Susan had arrived to stay.

Aunt Susan spoke for her. 'Everybody has a mother, Charles,' she said. 'But Mamma's mother had to go away when Mamma was very young. That sometimes happens. And then it's best not to talk about such things, because it makes people sad, and usually it's best not to talk about sad things. You would be sad if your mother went away, wouldn't you?'

'Oh yes,' he said, but sounded unconvinced. 'Though I suppose it would depend on where she went, for her sake, I mean. If she was going somewhere very nice she might be *contente* to have a little *repos*.' He had the habit of mixing French words with the English ones. It was because he spent so much time talking to the servants. This had worried Helen but Henry assured her that he would learn to speak French perfectly, as well as he spoke English, and would have no trouble in keeping the languages apart as he grew older.

Then he asked another of his questions. 'Mamma,' he

said, 'is Miss Gordon coming to live with us? What does it mean, being my governess?'

'Hard work, I would say,' said Aunt Susan, and the grown-ups laughed.

'It means,' said his mother, 'that she will look after you and give you your lessons and make you ready for when you have to go to school in England, when you are eight or nine years old.'

'*Elle est très gentille, Miss Gordon,*' he said seriously. '*Je l'aime bien. Je préférerais rester ici, Maman, qu'être obligé . . .*'

'Speak English, darling,' he was told. 'You're an English boy, not a French one.'

'Yes, I must exercise my English,' he said, and again they laughed, so that he looked puzzled and hurt. 'Was that funny? Why was it funny?' he asked, but they would not tell him. Then he had another question. 'Mamma, are you older than Papa? I thought mothers were usually younger than fathers.'

She was older, though only by three years. What should she say to her perspicacious son? Why must he ask these awkward questions? How did he know that she was older than Henry? Had the servants told him, did she look older? How many people knew or guessed? Surely she looked younger than he did? Hardly anyone had seen her pass-port... they were always careful in conversation to keep details of her early life vague, not that it was dubious...

'Yes, my darling, a little,' she said.

He was still looking at her in that enquiring way when Aunt Susan spoke with her usual decisiveness. 'On the whole,' she said, 'it is a bad idea to ask anyone their age unless they are very young. And no one ever asks a woman her age.'

'Not even their own mother?' he wondered. 'So that one knows the facts?'

'Not even their own mother.'

'I'm sorry, Mamma, if I have been *impoli,*' he offered. 'I did not mean to be. But it seemed to me to be important to find out the truth.'

Not answering, she took up *A Little Princess*, the book they were enjoying at that moment. Though she started her reading with a page she had read the day before, Charles judged it best not to tell her. After a while Miss Gordon came into the room and stood, close to the door. 'Do sit down, Miss Gordon, please, we would like you to feel as though you were in your own home here,' she said, interrupting her story. And then she read on. ' "If Sara had been a different kind of child, the life she led at Miss Minchin's Select Seminary for the next ten years would not have been at all good for her. She was treated more as if she were a distinguished guest at the establishment than as if she were a mere little girl. If she had been a self-opinionated, domineering child, she might have become disagreeable enough to be unbearable through being so much indulged and flattered. If she had been an indolent child, she would have learnt nothing..." ' It did not occur to her, as she read, that the words might very well be applied to the only child of a wealthy manufacturer from Staffordshire who had been abandoned by his wife and who, coldly and remotely, lavished his wealth on his daughter.

She read, they all thought, very well. The lamp beside her shone on what was thought of as her Titianesque hair and on her white dress as she sat coiled in the blue armchair. Otherwise only the flickering light from the fire illuminated the room, playing on the hearth-rug and the Turkey rug in front of the sofa. Charles, engrossed again as they moved on to an unfamiliar part of the story, burrowed his head into the cushion he was supposed to sit on, while his brother, imperturbably good-humoured, created lofty, swaying piles of bricks which from time to time collapsed on to the floor.

On the other side of the fireplace, Aunt Susan, her back unfailingly erect, contemplated the woman whom she had brought up. This almost-child of hers, now seemingly dedicated to motherhood and domesticity, was more confident now than she had been in her childhood, but still uncertain, in need of guidance and comfort. Happy though Helen appeared to her aunt, it was a pity that she still seemed so anxious, so easily disturbed by trivial events. But on the other hand Helen was seemingly delighted by the life of Mentone, valetudinarian though it was, and glad to immerse herself in its busy society. She was already planning her At Homes and other entertainments.

From the shadows near the door, the silent, observant Miss Gordon watched them all, admiring the elegant unassuming comfort with which they surrounded themselves. She had been there less than two days but she did not look backwards, hardly thinking of the quiet life at home in Aberdeen that she had left. Rather, she wondered whether it was in this house and with this family that she would live and work, and whether she would settle in the South of France. It might seem an unexpected place for a daughter of Aberdeen, but had not many of her countrymen and women made their lives successfully away from home? Would the Williamsons become a second family for her, as she hoped they might? Or did the glimpse she was now enjoying of tranquillity and order beside this hearth represent a happiness to which she would only be admitted as employee and outsider – and only briefly perhaps, before the family needed domestic arrangements that excluded her? On the other hand they were so kind and anxious to welcome her, treating her as a person whose views were important, concerned to know the range of her reading so that they could be sure that she would give their children's education the best possible start. To Miss Gordon the figure of the fair and tender mother, reading intimately to her son, himself so sensitive and sweet-natured, seemed to represent the perfection of family life. She would be happy, she was sure, with these people.

During the reading, Henry entered the room. Seeing the three women and the children almost motionless in the light of the lamp and fire, only his wife swaying a little as she read and raising a hand to warn him not to speak, he felt for a moment that he was viewing a domestic genre painting by a Dutch master, Vermeer perhaps, or by that clever artist Wilson Steer. Happily, the interior that he was looking at was not a fiction, enclosed in a frame, but an image that existed in space, with no confining definition, in which he too played an important part. It would be a happy domestic one, he hoped: even though he had abandoned his professional ambitions, which had meant so much to him in his youth, he could at least hope to be a successful husband and father.

Many years later Charles tried to paint from memory a scene such as this, one of many evenings when he emerged from the nursery to be read to by their mother. He recalled vividly the soft firelit colours in the room, the light around his mother, her soft clear voice, the aura that seemed to surround her. But he could not re-create what he remembered, the painting never worked. As he tried to paint, the image that at first shimmered so brightly before his mind's eye was always fractured — by tears, was it, by memories of the anxieties and disappointments of later years?

⸺ 8 FEBRUARY 1914 ⸺

Letter from Miss Betty Gordon to her elder sister,
Mrs Abercrombie, in Aberdeen

Lou Paradou,
Mentone,
8 February 1914

Dear Bobbie

I must apologise for being such a poor correspondent, but with all the excitement of moving into this new position I have scarcely found a moment to sit down and write a letter, and I wanted to be sure I knew what I thought about the place and the people before writing. Well, I always said I would like to see the world beyond the dear old city of Aberdeen. I've certainly found contrast here. My feeling is — and you know I don't reach such conclusions rashly — that I have struck gold. These are the nicest and kindest people you could find. Mr Williamson had to retire early from his important job in the Indian Civil Service. He is quiet when you first meet him, I suppose shy, but extremely clever and well-read, much interested for some reason in my own reading (which is slender though he's impressed by my familiarity with the novels of Balzac and Flaubert!). He's very humorous and loves puns and comic verse and all sorts of droll things, plays with the children for hours. He tends to tease his wife a good deal though I'm not sure that she always knows it or even likes being teased when she realises that's what he's doing. They seem very united, and look after each other, fussing about being delicate and taking pills together and not overtiring themselves. I suppose that's the way they have to live. But they have a good deal of fun all the same, and play practical jokes, and lark about, and entertain a great deal. Her Sunday At Homes are very important events in the life of British Mentone.

Mrs Williamson is so welcoming to me that I wonder whether she's been longing for a woman companion. She said to me a day or two ago, 'You feel like the sister I never had.' This was very kind though I was a trifle surprised, having known her for scarcely more than a month. They make it plain that they're happy with me and treat me as though I were a member of the family. They also pay me rather well, unlike a member of the family, though there's nothing to spend money on here other than postcards and gowns, neither of which much interest me. I suppose I could gamble a great deal at Monte Carlo, or I could send you all huge boxes of French chocolates — well, that would certainly animate life in your well-conducted household and probably provoke Mr Abercrombie into discourses on resisting the flesh. They say they hope very much I'll stay though they're too thoughtful to take it for granted. But I'm sure I will, at least until the little boys are old enough to go to school, when no doubt I will pack my bags and take up duties in some grim house in England or Scotland.

The little boys are five and two, and adorable. The elder is called Charles, very clever, quiet, prone to surprise one. Rather withdrawn, I think, and shy of me when I arrived. That didn't last long, I'm happy to say – it's fortunate in my chosen profession (though what choice was there, one might ask?) that I like little boys and I suppose girls too. The younger is Francis, sweet and easy and affectionate and ready to put his arms around me the moment he met me. He is a wee bit young to be in the charge of a governess! But we contrive to pass the time well enough.

The house and garden are quite beautiful, and I wish you could see them, like Paradise, with a great view of the sea below and the mountains looming enormous behind. Mrs W is very busy in the garden which keeps her amused. And the servants (with whom I practise my rather rusty French) are as nice as can be. It seems to me a very happy house (and absurdly luxurious, not reminiscent of home in that respect!). I'm sure I shall be happy here. You will be gratified to hear that there is a Scottish church where I am to be seen weekly in February in the decorous little dress which I used to wear in high summer in Aberdeen, praying mightily and not at all setting my bonnet at the elderly gentlemen who smile at me as we say goodbye to the minister.

I miss all my darling family, and I miss you most, my dearest sister, and think often of our talks and your good counsel to me and your support in times of doubt. I miss many things about Aberdeen, much as I used to complain about how cold and dark it is. But one cannot cling to one's past and I am sure I was right to come here and gain new experiences, and I shall be back to see you all, I hope very soon. They shut up the house in the summer and go to England so perhaps I shall be released for a day or so!

There seems already to be a tendency here to rely on me . . . 'Oh, Betty will know . . . Betty will sort that out.' I can't imagine what makes them think I'm so reliable, you know what a giddy girl I was until very lately, but it's nice to feel I'm useful and sensible now that I'm a sober matron of twenty-eight.

With very much love to all of you
from your affectionate French governess sister
(I hope that sounds just a trifle wicked)

Betty

'HENRY, I'm so frightened by it all.'
'You've no need to be frightened for yourself, my darling. You're not going to be called up. No more am I.'

'But everything will be so much disturbed. Do you think it will be over in a few weeks, as they say, with a glorious victory?'

'I don't know about the few weeks or the glorious victory. Germany is very strong and well-armed and just as rich as we are. I think a great deal will depend on whether the Americans come into the war. Let's hope it will be on our side. But I don't think you need be frightened, lovey darling, any more than anyone must allow themselves to be frightened at such a time.'

'But suppose the Germans win the war, what then? Will life be made unendurable for people like us? Will there be a revolution? Will we be forced to go home?'

'My dear, nobody knows, probably not even God. I suppose He must be feeling pretty confused about the whole thing Himself.'

'Should we go back to England? I don't at all want to go back, especially now when we've just settled here so comfortably. It would be terrible for your health, in winter. But might we be arrested if we stayed in France? And what about our money — will we be able to get money out?'

'No reason to suppose not. I think we should stay put. We're as safe here as we would be anywhere. If we lived in Strasbourg, that would be different. But we don't.'

'You mustn't think, Henry, that it is your duty to go and volunteer for some sort of war work in England. That may be what you'd like to do, but you are just not strong enough for it, remember. You must think about yourself first, you know.'

Silence.

'Henry!'

'Yes, my love, of course. But I shall feel pretty aimless, just sitting here and drinking tea right through these events. I understand that in London everyone is delirious with excitement, especially the young. After all, we're not so old ourselves'

'They don't know what it is to lose someone they love. Henry, will you promise to stay in Mentone? I need you here, lovey darling, and the boys need you. You can't risk everything to live in London and have your lungs destroyed. It's your duty to stay here. I'm sure we could do something useful in Mentone. Henry?'

'Yes, my love, I know you're right, you're always right.'

'Do you think Betty will stay with us? I should be devastated if she left. And will we be allowed to keep the servants?'

'We have no menservants of military age. I don't think that will be a problem.'

'But you'll promise me to stay here, Henry darling, and not force me to go back to England in the winter, unless the Germans invade France and capture Paris?'

'Yes, yes, I expect I'll stay. I expect we'll all stay. I expect we'll all be very comfortable.'

⊰ JANUARY 1915 ⊱

WELL, IT WAS TO BE TEA, she decided, tea rather than lunch as Henry had proposed. The advantage of tea was that the timing was clear. The officers would arrive at four and at six, after a walk in the garden and a game of croquet if the poor young men were strong enough, they would know (at least, she hoped they would) that it was time to go, since if invited to tea one did not stay after six because one's hosts would have to attend to other things and then dress for dinner. Not that they really dressed, but they had to tidy themselves and she always changed her frock. Whereas lunch was much more complicated and meant everyone sitting round a table and her only being able to speak properly to one or two guests and the officers might not be sure when they were supposed to leave. Anyway, tea was easier for the cook, who had so much to deal with and found it difficult to create interesting meals with the limited provisions in the market.

Henry insisted for a while that an invitation to lunch would be more friendly and this upset her, but when she explained how formality should be avoided on such an occasion he understood.

The officers, six of them and all British on this first occasion, arrived punctually at four o'clock. They came on foot, having been dropped off at the end of the drive. They were not very seriously wounded, she was glad to see, though one of them had his arm in a sling and another limped. They all seemed very nice and indeed presentable, she thought, as she leant over the balcony to wave in welcome. A house custom had arisen when visitors arrived – though they did not have many visitors at present, since it was hardly decent to entertain now, unless in the most modest way, the English chaplain always being an exception, and the Scottish one too if he weren't so impossible. The custom was that she waved at visitors as they arrived, from the balcony of the *petit salon*. As they entered the hall, Victorine the parlourmaid would show them to the *cabinet de toilette*, where they were asked to wash their hands with a special lavender soap which her doctor, a most trustworthy man, had assured her was absolutely reliable as a disinfectant. Then they were asked to gargle, each guest being provided with his or her own glass, and a little measure of gargle mixture being poured into it from a bottle. Victorine would explain that Madame was delicate and expressed the hope that visitors did not mind doing this. According to Victorine, whom in the early days she had questioned on the matter, no one raised any objection. (In the case of arrivals who were rapidly judged by this astute domestic to be exceptionally important or potentially difficult the hand-washing was waived, though Mrs Williamson never knew this.) And once guests had washed away the dirt and the germs of the outside world, they were shown upstairs.

On this occasion there was a pause, since washing took a while and the officers wanted to come upstairs as a group. They laughed a good deal as they did it, though more than one reflected that if their hostess had seen them in the state they had been in a month or so earlier, or some of the things that had passed through their hands, she would never have wanted to receive them at all. Finally ready, they advanced upstairs, falling without thought into the order of their seniority.

Mrs Williamson had dressed with some care, not wanting her guests to be disappointed over this opportunity to recall a world of grace and feminine beauty from which they had been excluded for such a long time. She wore white, with a blue sash, quite old clothes since one could hardly buy new ones at this time (though some Frenchwomen were less than scrupulous in this way, perhaps anxious to secure husbands when eligible men were becoming scarce). The dress had seemed a little tight when she tried it on a day or two before but Emma, her maid, had solved that problem. Beside her was a parasol, which she thought might be useful and indeed look pretty when they were making the garden walk, which must be part of the proceedings. As they waited, rather silent, Henry sat opposite her looking, she thought, uncomfortable. Why should he be ill at ease when they were behaving with such kindness to officers of His Majesty's Forces whom they scarcely knew, and striking a blow, though it had to be admitted a relatively modest and comfortable one, for the future of civilisation? And after all, she and Henry were about to embark on war work of their own.

Finally the door opened and Victorine came in, very serious, then smiled in that endearing way she had, deferential and yet affectionate. 'Madame, les invités,' she offered, as though not sure how to introduce six officers of the British Army, convalescent in her native territory, none of whose names or faces she knew any more than her employers did.

Mr and Mrs Williamson stood to greet their guests and the moody anxiety that had hung in the room for a moment evaporated. The occasion was immediately a success. Who could be shy when the hosts expressed themselves with such warmth, looked with such kindness into the eyes of each guest? The Williamsons so enthusiastically repeated that in this house their guests must consider themselves in a corner of England that the visitors, disposed anyway to enjoy the occasion, soon lost any feelings of reserve.

Major Pearson, at thirty-five the eldest and most senior of the arriving officers was generally curious about people and the surroundings they chose for themselves. To him, longing as he was for his wife and remembering at all too many bitter-sweet moments her smiling sidelong glance, the Williamsons and the room in which they stood epitomised the happiness of domesticity, from which for long months he and his brother officers had been excluded. The room his hosts had created for themselves was pretty, with its green-striped wallpaper setting off the pictures in their gilded frames, the painted ceiling, the curtains in buff-coloured linen that stretched almost to the ground, the Oriental rugs on the polished wooden floor. They had chosen comfortable furniture, English in feeling, with armchairs and sofas upholstered in floral fabric. Here and there were things they must have bought in France, such as the pair of little chandeliers in front of the looking glass. He held back as the others greeted his host and hostess, and lightly studied the pair (as he had learnt unobtrusively to do over many years in the Army) as they made their welcomes. The man was about his own age, in his mid-thirties, fair, very English, intelligent, well-bred. He was wearing a rather old and well-cut grey suit. He was asthmatic, they had been told, but looked perfectly well. As for the woman, she was perhaps a little older than her husband, not beautiful but amiable, pinkish in the face, smiling, an accomplished hostess, knowing what to do in these slightly unusual circumstances, interested in her guests. 'John Pearson,' he said, when his turn came.

'I'm glad you don't all click your heels like the Germans,' she remarked to him.

'Oh,' he replied, 'our manners aren't really modelled on the Germans', you know.'

'I've never shaken hands with so many officers in a row,' she said.

'We don't goose-step either. I tried once but I fell over,' said one of the very young men. 'In fact some of us hardly know how to keep in step on parade. I certainly don't, can't remember which is my left foot and which is my right.' He looked like a schoolboy, blond and fresh-faced, only there were unexpected lines around his eyes.

'Oh, you've got two left feet, so there's no problem,' one of his friends offered.

'It's very kind of you to visit us,' she told them. 'We thought you would like to see the view from the terrace before we went down to tea.'

The view scored heavily when they trooped on to the balcony and had the sights in their sights, as they put it. When they had suitably exclaimed over the view for several minutes the party went downstairs to the drawing room. There, tea appeared on trays and on little stands which could hold three or four plates at a time ('We call them curates in our family,' said Mrs Williamson, 'do you?'): the best Royal Worcester (seldom used these days, because of the war), and China tea and Indian tea and cucumber sandwiches and a lemon cake and a slightly pinched version of a fruit cake and éclairs, which Mrs Williamson assured them had been made expressly for them. The visitors seemed almost overcome. The food at the hospital, they said, was very sustaining and much better than anything offered on active service — not that their hosts would want to hear about that, of course — but it was not exactly a pleasure. Whereas this was delicious and so like being at home again. She thought that one of them was almost weeping as he stared at the scones Miss Gordon had made, though with great difficulty, proper flour being almost unobtainable. Two of the officers were only nineteen or so and Mrs Williamson realised with mild shock, not seeing many people of that age at present, how much older she was than they. She looked after these two with particular care, piling their plates with the chaste delicacies of her kitchen and asking them where they came from and when they had last seen their mothers, eager to comfort them and glowing in the realisation that she was able to give them, if only for a moment, a recollection of feminine affection.

When tea was fully under way, Miss Gordon came into the room with the two boys. Mrs Williamson introduced her to the guests, finding that she could already remember almost all their names. 'This is Miss Gordon,' she said, 'who is the children's governess and she's our governess too, really, she keeps us all in order. I cannot imagine life without Miss Gordon. And she made the scones too.' Miss Gordon smiled and said, reducing the encomium to an appropriate level, 'I hope you like the scones. Nothing is more difficult to make in France at any time, but especially now. But to you, such problems can hardly seem significant.'

There was silence for a moment, each reminded of the impact that the war had made on their own lives (or in the case of Henry, his wife thought, had blessedly not made). The officers stopped eating, as though to wolf an éclair as they had been doing with unobtrusive persistence would be to denigrate these problems. At length Major Pearson remarked agreeably, 'When I'm at my most uncomfortable, the thought of one of these days having a good meal — and a hot bath, actually — is about the only thing that sustains me. Much more than patriotism, I'm afraid.' He said it with a laugh in his voice to show he was being ironic (it was a surprising thing to say, Helen thought), and continued, 'And the thought that though scones are hard to make they are still attainable is extremely reassuring.' They all laughed and Miss Gordon and Mrs Williamson tried to offer the plates of cakes to the guests but the two youngest — this was, after all, the British Army that was visiting — rose hastily and prevented them.

Meanwhile the two little boys, dressed for the occasion in sailor suits, were standing by the door and gazing at the visitors. 'This is Charles and Francis,' said their father. 'Go round and shake hands with our guests.' Which the boys did solemnly, one after the other, until one of the officers produced a handkerchief from his pocket and made it into a rabbit. From such a mighty person this was even more unexpected and funny than it would have been from a usual sort of person. Meeting these soldiers, who they were sure must all be heroes, was the most exciting thing that had ever happened to them.

The Williamsons did not ask their guests about the war. How could they? Nor did they enquire much about their time in Mentone, or how long they expected to be there, since such questions would remind them that they were unwell and might never fight again. Henry wanted to talk about the war, and the experience of fighting, and the trenches, and how long the conflict might last, but he could hardly involve these wounded men in a discussion of their wartime life. It would be a cruel reminder of their suffering, he supposed, though one was not supposed to think in such terms. So they kept their talk to the house, and the garden, and the work of the Patriotic League of Britons Overseas of which Henry was a local committee member, and whether or not any of them would like to play tennis while on the Riviera, which could easily be arranged since Henry was president of the Lawn Tennis and Croquet Club. They did enquire about home. Major Pearson, it seemed, was a professional soldier who had been about to retire to run his estate in Dorset when the war broke out; another was, or had been, a schoolmaster at Harrow, and one was a banker, and one very young man had hardly done anything before joining the Army. Among them was a composer, who had written a number of songs, and orchestral pieces, many of which had been performed. 'Not much chance of compos-ing on active service,' he said, 'and I don't think I could get very far with music for military bands.' Henry and Helen, who were always attracted by people involved in the artistic life, were both drawn to this quiet, compelling man.

Helen told the officers that she and her husband were shortly to start working — helping, as Henry swiftly amended the description — in the Hospital of the Entente

Cordiale, recently established in the former Imperial Hotel. 'We are so relieved,' she said, 'to be able to help in a small way towards the war effort.'

'And you're also helping the war effort by having us to tea,' said Major Pearson. 'Believe me, that's a proper contribution too. I can't tell you how much it cheers us all up to come into a proper English house, and be made so welcome.' He would have liked these people to be his friends, real friends, not friends in the artificial sense induced by these peculiar circumstances. When he went back to the trenches, would he ever see people like this again – unless he had one more opportunity to go home and be reminded of the possibility of being happy? The man was particularly sympathetic, though he seemed ill at ease. Was it his wife who made him uneasy? Was it the reminder that his military visitors gave him of the war, and of the suffering from which he was so strangely exonerated?

The final moments for decent consumption of tea being over, they went into the garden. January could be a beautiful time of year in Mentone, and this year it was. The garden had been lovingly cultivated in the past months by the old gardener, who had come with the house, and his boy Franco, still only fourteen, who had just been employed (and who, Mrs Williamson hoped, would never have to go to war). Although they had not been able at such a time to make many structural changes, the terraces had been tidied and replanted and a lawn sown on the lowest level. It was hardly an English lawn, but with proper attention it looked passable. A new rectangular pool had been created, and she had planted quantities of irises, white iris on one terrace and purple on the one below, though these would not flower yet awhile.

They admired the mimosa, they admired the winter buddleia. She was glad to see the young men smile as they walked along the paths, hardly speaking for a while. She did not talk much, thinking they would not welcome it. 'Every sense is delighted here,' said the major, rather sadly, as though his mind were elsewhere. 'It reminds me of home a bit, though my own garden is much less splendid. My wife loves it, and works away at it, and it looks pretty nice in June when it's not raining. But this is wonderful — you've created an English garden in France. Very clever of you, Mrs Williamson.'

Of the second lieutenants, one was fair-haired, one browner, both with an edge of tension around their mouths. But they were boyish enough. One pointed excitedly at the pool and said, 'Look, goldfish, just like the ones at home. Don't leap in after them, Charlie.' They stood and looked at the sea and the mountain, and the two of them speculated on how long it would take to climb the mountain and said to her banteringly that they expected she climbed it often herself and how long did it take? She was pleased they felt they could tease her.

Henry had not said much for a while, and when she looked closely at him she saw that he was abstracted, almost pained, nearing — she could generally though not infallibly read his emotions — the state of silent misery that some-times assailed him for no reason she ever understood. He noticed her and his expression changed. He smiled towards her and frowned to himself and addressed a question to the officer next to him.

The men stayed for a long while, until the sun disap-peared over the horizon, talking a good deal, insisting on being shown every corner of the garden and asking her eagerly about her plans for its improvement. She explained that she wanted as far as possible to create an English garden beside the Mediterranean or at least a garden which would combine the best of English and southern traditions. Henry, she was relieved to see, had engaged the major in conversation about a further German push. 'Is it possible that they could break through?' Henry asked, to which the major answered, 'Anything is possible, sir' – though why 'sir' when Henry was hardly older than he was . . . Perhaps it was intended as a courtesy. How was it possible that the Germans could break through the British and French defences? 'I should love to come and paint here,' said one of the visitors, and she thrilled at this prospect, urging him to come as often as he wished, thrusting out of her mind the thought of war. War had no place in her *hortus conclusus*, closed to the world but opened to her friends. This was her enchanted refuge, enriched by the views of sea and town and mountain and yet happy in its privacy; it was a place no one could spy on. What premonition could she have, on that day of spring sunshine among the olive trees, of the final shattering impact that another war would make upon her, so many days away, so many hours of teas and comfort and books, of tennis and amateur theatricals and sociable plans and laughter, of undiscussed fear and frustrations and unhappiness?

They finally left after it had grown dark, with numerous apologies for having stayed so long and anxieties expressed about how strict Matron would be with them when they returned, and how she might send them to bed with no supper. 'That would be something to be grateful for,' said one of the youngest men, and they all laughed. They must come again very soon, the Williamsons insisted, the next week if possible, and whenever they wanted to walk or sit in the garden or come to tea they would be extremely welcome. They would all still be in Mentone the following week, would they not? They left waving and laughing with a freedom that was quite different from their respectful manner when they arrived, and Mrs Williamson turned to her husband and said, 'They were quite charming, weren't they?'

'Yes,' he replied. 'I am very glad they came. I'd have liked to ask them more about the war. But one can't, I suppose.'

'No,' she replied, 'one must not talk about unpleasant things when offering hospitality.'

They had dinner rather quietly and went to bed without reading aloud or playing cards as they normally did. Helen was glad that the day had gone well, and glad that in only a few days she and Henry would begin their own war work at the French hospital.

⟶ RECOLLECTIONS ⟵

For the boys, the war seemed like an adventure. Their governess showed them maps of France and Russia and explained how the armies were moving around northern Europe, and what the trenches were. When her charges asked her whether the Germans were devils, she replied that she had never been to Germany and so could not judge, but she believed on the whole that they were people much like themselves, and after all the King's family were German, too. When asked why the war was being fought, she conceded that the Germans had invaded Belgium, but not much more. She did not talk about the trenches or the slaughter but she did convey to them, subtly as Charles later realised, that war was evil and in no way exciting.

Still, it was immensely exciting when real soldiers turned up at the house. Charles had often seen photographs in the illustrated papers of our British soldiers and, of course *Punch* was filled with comic depictions (and occasional heroic ones) of fighting men, but never until the beginning of 1915 had he seen them in the flesh. When he first glimpsed a group of officers in the *petit salon*, they seemed to him enormous, magnificent, their khaki infinitely more heroic than the armour worn by the knights in armour in his picture books, their shoulder flashes and Sam Brownes (as he knew them to be called) redolent of martial prowess. It was rather disappointing that they were drinking tea and eating scones, but he supposed his mother could not have been expected to provide the flagons of beer and sides of beef which soldiers surely preferred to feast on. As he gazed at them, clutching his little brother's hand for reassurance, he was startled to find that these wonderful men spoke English, and smiled in a jolly way. One of them knelt down to talk to him, and made a rabbit out of his handkerchief, which leapt up his arm in a very funny way when Charles stroked it and perhaps was a rabbit after all. The boys were sent round the room to shake hands with all these huge cheerful officers, aware that their parents and Betty were watching them. How many guests were there? Dozens and dozens, it seemed.

In the following months visits by the military became a regular event. Nurses and doctors came too, but they were not so interesting. The nurses had an annoying way of asking him about his lessons whereas the officers usually asked him about his games. The boys always begged to be allowed to say hello to the officers, and though Betty would tell them that the gentlemen did not want to talk to children, she always gave way. Many years later, Charles found photographs of himself and his brother, usually in sailor suits, which still looked acceptable, though the floppy hats their mother insisted on now seemed absurd. They would be standing with a group of soldiers on the lawn, sometimes lifted on the men's shoulders, or sitting on their knees at tea, with everybody smiling broadly and tidily posed. Charles had his favourites among the visitors. He soon learnt that affection brought its penalties when the officer he liked best of all did not reappear and he was told that Captain Rawsthorne had gone back to war. Would he be coming back? Well, perhaps one day, they said, and he knew that meant no. He remembered vividly in later years the reassurance of sitting on the knee of a demi-god, held securely in place by a mighty arm, and being given more bites of cake than he would ever get in the nursery.

It was a happy time for the little household, as Charles recalled. His mother and father were always busy, intrigued by the glimpses that the hospital and the soldiers gave them of a larger world. They spent a good deal of time with their children, all the same, and though Charles knew instinctively that his mother preferred Francis to himself, he accepted this (or so he thought) as somehow a part of life. But it was the heroism of the officers that interested him most. Would he grow up to be like them? he used to ask Betty. Would he ever be so large and brave? And she would laugh, and say, 'After this war there will be no more wars and you will never need to be a soldier.' Still, he always suspected that she was wrong, and that soldiers would always be needed. He wondered sometimes if she looked sad on the afternoons when Major Pearson visited, after he had gone away.

➤➦ 8 FEBRUARY 1915 ➥➤

Letter from Miss Gordon to Mrs Abercrombie in Aberdeen

Lou Paradou,
8 February 1915

Dear Bobbie

Thank you for your interesting letter, and I am glad to
hear that you remain cheerful in the face of so many
difficulties.

You ask me about myself. I have been thinking very
deeply, as you can imagine, about what I should be doing
at this overwhelming moment in the history of our
nation and the world. Since I am still quite young and
could perhaps make some contribution, however modest,
to the war effort, I have naturally been wondering
whether I should abandon my hardly arduous duties here
at Lou Paradou and come home and work as a nurse or
in the Civil Service. I am tempted to come, since I find
it uncomfortable to be spending this time in the sunny
comfort of Mentone, when so many people are enduring
danger and hardship both in the trenches and at home.
There's no denying, life here is still very pleasant, and of
course the sun shines as sweetly as it did before war
broke out, and the servants are all still here (though the
cook left and it took a little while to find a new one —
this was considered a catastrophe in our well-ordered

household!). We, or rather I should say 'they', though it feels like 'we', do not have huge lunch parties in the pre-war way, but there is still much social activity. In particular the Ws are very busy entertaining wounded soldiers who are convalescing in the town. I feel so sorry for them, poor young men, being fattened up to go back to the front — though of course I can't say so. They seem to love coming here and the Ws are extremely kind and welcoming and surely enjoy meeting such a number and variety of people, some of them very interesting. And they are friendly too with some of the doctors and nurses from the English hospital here. I think our visitors find Lou Paradou like heaven (did you know, the name means 'Paradise' in the local dialect?). Mrs W looks so well and happy at the centre of this little world, it does me good to see her.

All the same I sometimes feel this is all a little too comfortable, particularly when I lie in bed in the morning and my tea is brought to me by Victorine and we chat about the day past and the day to come. But after much thought I have decided to stay, at least for the time being. I feel I am useful here, and important, and though Mrs W is in very good form at present I have a feeling (which I've rather tended to resist) that I've already become very necessary to her and that my departure would be damaging. Is it mistaken to feel that I have a duty to private individuals at a time like this, a greater duty than to my country? I don't know. And I'm very devoted to the little boys, who are as affectionate and naughty and sweet as any children could be. Of course, there is no proper school for them so they are very dependent on me, and their parents, for their education. Reading is going pretty well for Charles who is as bright a child as I've ever met, and I don't think I am just being partial here. And Francis looks pretty promising, too. I shall miss them when they are too old for the school-room, for all sorts of reasons.

The fact that I am happy here is not necessarily a reason why I should give Mentone up, is it? What do you think, you wise old thing? If you feel I ought to come home and learn to be a nurse or an elementary teacher, well, then I will, and Mrs W and her children will have to look after themselves. I suppose that at such a time private considerations must be sacrificed – and by private considerations I mean caring for individuals, private people, rather than people engaged in combat. Perhaps I should say that I do work two days a week in the hospital, so I am not entirely idle.

Reading the death lists in *The Times* is a really horrid duty. Thank God no one important to us has been killed yet. I know it's wicked of me, but I was very relieved that Archie M. escaped with a leg injury which means he can't go back to the front. I know I should be disappointed that he can't now die for his country, but I'm not. Mr W and I talk about the war a great deal, in a guarded sort of way, and I think we agree in our views of it, or at least over the impossibility of reaching a view. He works very hard on all sorts of charities for the wounded and so on, but I think he feels uneasy about being here, you can't help it if you are of military age. She is more loyal and unquestioning. I know your feelings, my dearest.

I think of you all often. I hope life is not too hard for you, and that you can keep yourselves properly warm and comfortable, and decently fed. Love to all, and not too much whisky.

Your loving sister
Betty

The most perfect hospital at Menton is without question the one now installed in the Hotel Imperial and called the Hospital of the Entente Cordiale. It is very doubtful if any other town on the Riviera has a hospital that can rival or even equal this one in comfort, with its vast airy wards and comfortable beds, in luxury with its hundreds of baths and beautiful surroundings, in the perfection of its appointments, in the equipment of its theatre, in the number of skilled doctors and trained nurses, and in the excellence of the general management.

Menton and Monte Carlo News, April 1915

⇥ NOVEMBER 1917 ⇤

LATER, HENRY OFTEN RECALLED THAT MOMENT, extracting it from his file of intimate memories. It was a day when they had both been working at the Entente Cordiale: they had gone there together in the morning by tram and had parted in a businesslike manner, as though they were really professional people with official occupations. He had set off to the X-ray department, where he carried out various humble but intricate duties for the doctors. She, already in her uniform with the cap bearing the Red Cross, had hurried to the ward on the third floor where she acted as 'marraine' or godmother to fifty wounded French soldiers. Being something of an invalid herself, she felt, as she sometimes told Henry, that she was particularly able to understand and sympathise with their weaknesses. All day she would talk to the soldiers, read their letters to them and write out those they dictated, hold their hands if they were unable to communicate in words, plump up their pillows, bring them drinks – most importantly of all, perhaps, talk to them about their families and girls and comrades lost in battle, and their imminent recovery (even if it was clear they would never recover), and listen to stories about their lives before the war. She hardly heard about their experiences in the trenches, not because she would have been unwilling to listen to anything she was told but because the men were too polite to burden this blonde angel with their troubles. Those who might have insisted were on another ward. She had taken the trouble to learn all their names, and when men left to return to their families or to be retrained for combat or to be buried, she did not forget them. For almost three years she had been working on the ward, and there was scarcely a man whose name escaped her.

The partitions between the old hotel rooms on her floor had been knocked down to create two long wards, white, cool and clean, with a row of windows on to the town's gardens and the sea. By the time they reached the hospital, the men were still ill or badly wounded, but seldom in a shocking condition. It was a fine and orderly place, filled with hope and movement and efficiency, where the doctors and the nurses moved with purposeful kindness among their charges. Occasionally she found herself wishing that she, too, could move with such professionalism between patients whose lives depended on her care. That could not be — but in the meantime, she was grateful that she could help to bring the happiness and relief she could sometimes see in the faces of her temporary charges.

After one of these days at the hospital, Henry awaited her in the huge marble entrance hall of the hotel-hospital, so that they could travel home. She was late, but this did not make him anxious: he knew she would often linger if someone wanted her to stay. Finally she emerged through one of the side doors. She seemed tired, and was wiping her forehead with her hand as she came into the room. She looked around the hall until she saw him standing by the main door, staring in her direction. Then she made a gesture he would never forget, deliberately recalling it years later at times when she tried his patience almost beyond endurance. It was a gesture of pleasure and mock-surprise: she raised her hands to the level of her shoulders, the palms towards him, the fingers stretched, and burst into a smile that transformed her again into the girl, fresh, eager, gay, vulnerable, whom he had courted twelve years before in England. For a second she paused and then hurried towards him, a little breathless, eager to kiss him and tell him about her day. He stood and waited for her. In his head he heard a voice, decisive and not to be argued with, which said to him, 'This is the woman you love, and with her your whole life will be spent.'

That was the version of the episode – trivial, yet to him memorable – he once recounted to Francis. Whether the voice also said to him, 'This is the woman with whom you will die,' we shall never know. He did not discuss that detail with his son.

⊰ APRIL 1918 ⊱

A LTHOUGH HELEN'S PLANS for major reconstruction in the garden were frustrated by the war and
the shortage of labour and materials, she spent as much time
as she could in planning for the future and in introducing
modest improvements that could be carried out by Luca and
Franco. At seventeen, Luca was still just too young to be
conscripted and she worried about him and his mother, who
had no other child, if the war continued. In the mornings
when she was not busy at the hospital she would make a
rendezvous with Luca at the front door, to inspect progress
and discuss plans. He was, she discovered, not at all
interested in innovation, regarding the garden as perfectly
acceptable in its present state. But unlike the head gardener
at Blithbury, who had chosen to obstruct any change almost
as a matter of principle, Luca would acquiesce in her ideas
with only the mildest expression of resignation.

The verandah, with its six columns supporting the
wisteria, stretched the length of the house and was an area
she particularly wanted to beautify. In her predecessor's day
the beds between the verandah and the drive had been
planted with the dullest of shrubs and only the wisteria
tumbling from the columns and crossbeams gave any pleasure. With a little advice from Henry (he preferred to be
invited to give his views when the major decisions had

already been made), she filled the beds with plants that reminded her as far as possible of England, purple and pink stocks set between rows of lavender. Along the terrace she introduced four large terracotta pots. Luca had found them for her, from a friend, he said. She wondered who this friend might be who possessed such handsome things and even whether the friend had found them in the garden of one of the large villas that had lain empty for much of the war, belonging to Swedes or Russians and, of course Germans, who could hardly find their way to Mentone during the conflict. Into these pots were introduced bedding-out plants, which Luca again procured from some mysterious source, she thought from an old friend of his in Ventimiglia who had run a large nursery garden before 1914 and still cultivated a few plants to keep himself entertained. They would change the plants two or three times each season, between late September when they moved back to the house, and the spring. In the summer, when they went away, the pots stayed empty.

From the verandah one reached the garden proper, and here Helen would walk when there was time. Her favourite spot, she thought, was the marble table under the pergola, which extended along the lawn. Sitting there she could study the pool under the largest of the olive trees, constantly replenished by the bronze boy from the mouth of the fish he held in his right hand. Behind this statue stretched the sea, almost always sparkling and constantly enthralling: even when it was grey and uninviting the hidden sun would sometimes etch a line of silver towards the horizon. Through the yellow banksia rose above the pergola she could glimpse the steeply sloping terraces, scattered with villas, pink and white and ochre. Above the green slopes rose the huge cliff, its rockface grey and tawny in the sun, black in the rain. Today it looked reassuring, she thought, like the wall of a castle, protecting her and her family from the cruel world beyond. At this little table, surrounded by cushions and workboxes (which she scarcely ever looked into, but they seemed to suggest womanly and faintly patriotic activity), her pen tray and a pile of newspapers and books, she spent many quiet moments, often alone but still at the centre of the house's activities.

It was there that she was sitting one morning in April 1918. Pleasant though the immediate situation was, with the sun justifying all the praises anyone had ever piled on the Mentone climate, this was a sombre time. Relieved by the withdrawal of Russia from hostilities, the Germans had launched a major offensive on the Western Front, and were enjoying frightening success. The hospitals in the town were fuller than ever, and the mood among some of the officers — even the nicest and most gentlemanly ones — was strangely unsettled and resentful. She later remembered this morning as one of the war's most painful moments. Victorine emerged from the house with the little cup of coffee Helen liked to drink in the middle of the morning and was followed by Betty.

Betty was not, as usual, calm and cheerful and friendly. Her face was red, her eyes were red, her mouth was taut but quivering. She was holding *The Times*.

There was only one explanation. 'Betty,' Helen said. 'Who is it?'

'It's Major Pearson,' Betty replied. 'John Pearson. Killed in action, 12 April 1918.'

'Oh, no,' she said, 'I'm so sorry. Such a nice man. Such a good friend.' For so he had been, during the months he had passed in the town at the beginning of the war, during the period of administrative duties he had spent there in 1916, and on the occasional later visits he had made to Mentone to see them. He had stayed with them this past Christmas, his wife having died in the meanwhile, nobody knew quite why. These tragedies, Helen reflected, surrounded them on every side – although they themselves seemed immune from disaster.

'Such a nice man, and almost forty, you'd think they could have let him off the fighting. Such a dear man...' and Betty burst into tears. She sat down at the table and when the boys, whom she had left for a moment at their lessons, ran out into the garden to find her, they were startled and shocked to find their imperturbable governess shaking and red-faced and dabbing at her eyes with a small moist handkerchief. Helen put her arm around Betty and held her hand, and told the children to run away and play in the garden. Betty soon recovered her composure. She stretched out her arms and clenched her fists and stood up. 'This terrible war,' she said, 'this terrible war...' And she returned to her duties.

⇥ 14 NOVEMBER 1918 ⇤

HENRY STOOD ON THE BALCONY and waited for the family to assemble. Armistice at last, and unexpectedly, and there was hardly a doubt that Armistice would lead to peace. English newspapers took days to reach Mentone but the French press was trumpeting the victory of the Allies (above all, of the French) and reporting troubling events in Germany, where the Kaiser had fled and revolution threatened. He looked gloomily at the editorial in *The Times*: 'We drew the sword without hatred or passion because Germany compelled us to draw it; but the inexpiable brutalities which she perpetrated so long as she had the power, and which no class of her people dared to condemn, have filled us with a loathing and a righteous indignation which will not readily pass away. She has been false and cruel. She must bear the penalty in our mistrust and in our abhorrence . . .' Well, yes, and must she? Was it wise, this attitude? Would it heal the suffering and the wounds created by the war?

From his terrace Henry could see on the front — it was, he thought ironically, the only front he had seen during the war — crowds of people swarming towards the Old Town. For four years the town had been so quiet, with scarcely a person moving along the pavements other than invalid soldiers and large numbers of Senegalese soldiers, stationed in temporary barracks in the town. These 'ebony warriors', as they were known in the English paper, were at first regarded with admiration as examples of the noble savage but all too soon resented. Now this somnolent place was suddenly pullulating with people. Where had these people been throughout the war? They waved tricolour flags and Union Jacks and Italian flags and sang national songs as they advanced towards the port with its toy castle where, in a few minutes, a cannon salute was to be fired. In the evening there would be fireworks, as there had not been for four miserable years.

The door from the *petit salon* opened and Betty Gordon appeared, wearing – the first time he had seen such a thing – a white dress with a tartan cockade on her breast. He bowed to her, acknowledging her finery with a gesture. She brought with her Charles, now nine years old and wearing the grey pinafore of the French schoolchild. He clung to her lovingly, but ran forward on seeing his father. Since September he had been a pupil at the *lycée* in Mentone: on account of the war it had been impossible to send him to the preparatory school in England to whose high-thinking discomfort successive generations of boys in the family had been consigned. Behind them, bouncing and with his face as always open to happiness, came his little brother Francis, now six. His schooling, unlike Charles's, was the subject of much discussion. Helen could hardly bear the thought of Francis having to leave them at eight years old. English schools, she claimed, were so demanding and then he was delicate (though there was no evidence of this, Henry considered, no child was less delicate nor had been better sheltered from dangers).

'Betty' he said, 'you do honour to Scotland.'

'And look, Pa,' cried Francis. 'I have a Union Jack, and so does Charles and we can't wave them at the King and Queen since they aren't here but perhaps we can wave them at Mr Wavertree.' Mr Wavertree was the English chaplain, and a man of impressive appearance both in and out of the pulpit.

'I am sure Mr Wavertree would be very pleased,' said his father, 'though he isn't quite the same as the King and Queen. I suppose, Betty, he will come and call and we shall need to celebrate somehow — what does Helen think?'

'She will be down in a moment,' Betty replied. 'I am sure she will have a plan.'

'Oh, yes, no doubt.' Odd how in moments of excitement it was so hard to abandon the usual preoccupations or discard irony about oneself. Intellectual excitement, at least, liberated one's spirit — though not much of it was available in Mentone. Why was he not more exhilarated? Why was he more conscious than ever of his deficiencies and his failure to contribute to the victory being celebrated so energetically in the streets?

One way or another Helen will have a plan for organising the day, and no doubt it will be a very good plan, he thinks, as she emerges from the house. She is wearing one of the white dresses which she liked before the war because they complement her complexion and her hair but which she gave up during the hostilities as unsuitably frivolous. The dress is, he thinks fleetingly, a shade tight in spite of the rigours of a wartime diet (which includes banishing cake except on Sunday or when patients and doctors from the hospital come to visit). But it is good to see her in holiday garb, smiling, and with a little Union Jack scarf fluttering round her neck.

'Darling,' she says. ' Here you are, and here all of us are, and I have told Victorine that they must all come up and we will drink some champagne.'

And here indeed comes Victorine bearing a tray that jingles with glasses. She is followed by the new Belgian cook Madame Amélie (cooks have been a problem during the war, always going off to nurse or cook for the Army or join their wounded husbands) with a bottle of his best champagne, hardly chilled but what does that matter? He must work harder on the first fine careless rapture or at least careless rapture *tout court* which is eluding him. Behind parlourmaid and cook come Emma, the lady's maid, and Alice, the housemaid, and the two gardeners. And looking at this boy, who if the war had continued would be going off shortly to be slaughtered, he feels at last the relief that has eluded him all morning, and to the surprise and pleasure of the little household on the balcony embraces his wife with gusto, indeed almost passion – an emotion seldom seen in that house.

'Henry!' she cries as best she can, startled by such exuberance. 'You'll crumple...' But, enraptured by the moment, he is kissing Betty Gordon, and then Victorine (kissing them, as he realises wryly, spontaneously but in order of precedence) and then the cook whose bosom is surprisingly warm and welcoming, a good thing in a cook, and then Emma, and then Alice, who always appears rather pale and sallow but whose body – which he has never thought about before – welcomes his hold and yet subtly resists it, a strange sensation and how odd that at such a moment he should notice it... Out of the side of his eye, meanwhile, he sees that his wife is confused by such behaviour, for which she has not been trained. She is unwilling to embrace her servants, or at least does not know how it should be done. Yet as the gun salute begins to fire in the harbour below, she feels it would be absurdly pale and English to shake their hands or wave at them like the Queen, and she is embarrassed. Luca, the old gardener, long used to employers and recalling the many pleasant hours he has spent with Madame discussing the garden, cannot let her stand immobile and undecided when all glimpse her unease. Stepping forward, he remarks, '*Madame permettra,*' in statement and not enquiry, and kisses her lightly on each cheek. The maids laugh, and follow his example, taking and pressing her hand as they do so, expressing in this kind gesture not only the drama of the moment but their affectionate fellow feeling as women. They kiss one another too while Henry, in his efficient mode, but gingerly, squeezes and pulls the champagne cork. It is a long time since they have drunk champagne. ·

As he struggles with the cork – is recalcitrance a sign of excellence in a champagne cork? he wonders – Henry finds himself thinking of the consequences of the peace for him. From a selfish point of view, the war has not been so bad, in spite of the general gloom and the occasional death of friends. It has been a pleasure to go two or three times a week to the hospital. He and Helen have often travelled over together in the car, or more often on the tram to save petrol. I suppose this will end, he thinks, in a few months or even less, since the hospital must close. Happy for them, sad for us.

The guns finally cease and from the harbour comes the sound of cheering. Henry pours more champagne, but there is scarcely more to pour, even for his expectant sons. There is a silence. More than one of them thinks how strange it is that they are standing here in a circle. The servants think of their own families, in Belgium, in Switzerland, in Avignon, or close at hand, with whom they might be celebrating this moment.

'You must have the day off,' says Helen, 'and celebrate.' When they protest, though not energetically, about lunch and dinner, she and Henry are firm. Miss Gordon will help them and they are not completely stupid. At such a moment (this she does not say, though she thinks it) all are equal in society, just as one day they would all be equal in death.

There is only one married woman there, Henry remembers, other than his own wife. And he turns to Madame Amélie, whose husband died in the fighting in 1916, and says, '*Vous avez perdu plus que nous tous.*' Upon which she bursts into tears, making Helen feel unworthy for allowing herself to worry about such trivial problems as preparing lunch. And is led away, Victorine wrapping her arm around the cook's waist. They hardly say goodbye to their employers in the strange emotion of the moment, leaving the family high on their balcony above the rejoicing town. Will they go and join the crowds, now or in the evening? No, on the whole not, think the Williamsons and Miss Gordon. They will stay in their eyrie and keep their feelings to themselves.

It is the peace, they all think. It is a new world. And in this new world we shall be happy, and never make the mistakes we made so often in the old one.

❦ RECOLLECTIONS ❧

WHEN CHARLES CAME BACK to the house after
the Second World War he hardly thought about his
parents' style of living, and when he was reminded of it
found no pleasure in the memory. In putting the house
together again he made no effort to re-create the formal
comforts that he remembered from childhood. Rather the
reverse: their way of life seemed irrelevant in the brave
post-war days of socialist reconstruction when the old order
was happily being consigned to the dustbin. He was intoxi-
cated by the opportunity to do what he liked with a place
that had often infuriated him in his youth. Besides which he
was a modernist, even if a tentative and sceptical one, and
had no interest in reconstructing an irrelevant past.

But though he might reject the past in theory, he could
not reject it altogether. A cloud of memories surrounded
him, and old sights, old conversations, old passions were
constantly reassembled in his mind. Some were prompted by
pieces of furniture that had survived the war. Some were
evoked by books. The books had almost all been left behind
by his parents when they moved to Pau, and had remained in
the villa while it was used by the Italian Army as an officers'
mess and later when it was empty or invaded by refugees.
Though gnawed in those last months by rats, presumably as
hungry as everyone else, the books had largely survived,

battered but still handsome, decorated with the artistic bookplates designed for his mother, which showed a river twisting into a rural distance.

Many of his memories were associated with corners of the house or the garden. As he walked and walked through his domain he glimpsed again a host of events, some still private to himself, some peopled and eventful. His images of childhood were usually associated with mornings. In recollection these were always clear and sunlit. They were suffused with the soft fragrance that filled the house when his mother allowed the windows to be opened on days when no possibility of a chill could be detected, physically or through the mediation of the *Nice-Matin*. If he selected an image from his early adulthood, the choice was smaller. He had been at the house less often then, and found it increasingly alienating. As he developed as a writer, with more and more of his articles accepted by *Horizon* and the *New Statesman*, and began to move among an interesting group of London intellectuals, his parents became less and less important to him. His new friends seldom talked about anything so irrelevant as parents, when the future of society, the non-viability of capitalism and the nature of art engrossed them. But on the rare occasions when they did touch on such trivially individual subjects, they would rapidly dismiss his people's existence in the South of France as self-indulgent and frivolous. He acknowledged that it was both of these things and and said that he agreed with them. But he knew too that it was neither, and never tried to explain the complexities of life at home to these passionate advocates of a socialist or Communist British republic. Nor was a discussion of life on the Riviera appropriate to the probing short story of working-class life in south London contrasted with wealthy life in Kensington, which was published in 1934 and began to establish his reputation.

A memory he liked to evoke in easier moods recalled the morning balcony outside the *petit salon*. Sometimes his family would have breakfast there. This happened less frequently as time passed, since his mother became ever less anxious to abandon her privacy, staying in her room until eleven or even noon, with only the passage of a tray piled with linen and silver to indicate that she was awake. But even if she was not with them, she could not let her family breakfast in unsuitable and even perilous circumstances. She would worry that the balcony, shaded by cypresses in the early part of the day, might retain the coldness of night. In the early days, when he still hoped that over matters of health she would be susceptible to reason, his father would argue that the temperature in the spring was never anywhere close to freezing and that the balcony would hardly ever be cold when the sun had risen. It never worked. Her fears (based on a notion she had picked up somewhere) that harmful vapours were retained in the atmosphere during the hours of darkness always prevailed. She would become agitated and reproachful, and Pa found it easier in the end to give way: over matters of health there was no persuading her. As the years passed they retreated to the dining room for all meals except tea, which by convention was consumed elsewhere. Tea on a warm day (as long as it was not too warm) might be taken on the balcony, under the protection of the awning, and otherwise in the *petit salon*. But in the early days, when his parents still cultivated enjoyment, breakfast on the balcony was a regular event.

When his schoolfriends from England came to stay, they found life at Lou Paradou unlike anything they were used to. At school he was teased for living in a villa, as the house was described in the list of boys' parents and addresses: a villa was one of those dreary little houses in yellow brick with a privet hedge on the outskirts of a provincial town, not a place where a fellow at one's school would live. Besides which, living in the South of France was strange enough, and not very English, and though they only teased him gently Charles did sometimes wonder whether his friends and their parents felt that abandoning Staffordshire for the South of France was quite the right thing for his people to have done. But on arrival his friends were charmed by the friendliness and individuality of his family and their house. For these boys, even breakfast at Lou Paradou was exotic compared to breakfasts at home. The white cups and saucers with their painted decoration of oranges and lemons and green leaves, the pottery of Mentone or the fine English china used on special days, all set out on a white tablecloth, pleased the eye in a way their own breakfast tables at home seldom did. The lightest of boiled eggs, exotically strong coffee of a sort they never drank at home, bowls of oranges and tangerines and kumquats, a strange little fruit one was expected to eat whole, skin and all. And on Sundays they were offered something called croissants, which never appeared in the halls and vicarages and terrace houses of their parents, oddly shaped like a half-moon and somehow both light and buttery. The croissant was named, they would be told by Charles's mater, after the crescent symbol of the Saracens and brought back by the Crusaders from the East.

At these early breakfasts – many such occasions drifting

into one sunny recollection – his parents would appear informally dressed and easy in manner. They would sit long over their coffee, his father looking at the French papers or *The Times* if a copy had arrived that morning, and his mother constructing plans for the day or sketching the guest list for a lunch party, discussing the day's menu in an airy way before her meeting with the cook. They held At Homes every first and third Sunday of the month, and these required a good deal of preparation in advance while supplying a huge amount of gossip afterwards. Betty Gordon would despatch her breakfast rapidly before setting off to deal with the house. This seemed to take much of her time, particularly after he and Francis had gone to boarding-school.

When there were friends to stay, breakfast assumed a more urgent character, since a programme of activity was often planned. The boys were to go swimming at the Rochers Rouges, the sheltered little bay just over the frontier. Or they would be having a picnic, or walking down the hill from Roquebrune (not a favourite activity of the young but enjoyed by their elders) or playing tennis at the Mentone Lawn Tennis and Croquet Club under the eye of Papa, or going for a drive in the mountains. These activities required a vast amount of planning from his mother in which his father, on appeal, would sometimes briefly but decisively join – but only sometimes, in spite of the constant solicitations of his wife.

On days of high organisation breakfast lacked the charm of mornings when nothing much was planned, and when he could play in the garden with his brother or, more often, on his own. On those mornings, his father and mother and he – and Francis, though he could not remember particularly what Francis got up to – would sit watching the harbour and listening to the mild activities of the household. Then, as a child, he would move on to the floor with its red tiles and play with his model castle and armies of medieval tin soldiers, fighting long battles in which all but two or three of the combatants would be killed. Meanwhile, his father would speak about the tennis club and its problems, and the dramatic society's next production, and sometimes the books he was reading. Occasionally he talked about the book on aspects of Greek society he was planning to write, and later was writing, and then somehow was writing no longer, or so it seemed. All this was very instructive when he was a little boy. Sometimes Charles and his father would talk at length. His mother tended increasingly to interrupt them with questions (often fired from the window of her bedroom, on the floor above) and worries that they should not sit too long in one place and that the sun was becoming too strong and the awning must be wound down. As Charles grew older and went to Eton he found that his father knew little about the outside world or the things that his friends at school would talk about, except what he derived from *The Times* and the occasional book. These conversations – 'our talks' as they were known – grew shorter and less frequent until they were silently abandoned. Only when he grew up did he realise that his father had sometimes tried modestly to revive them but, faced by Charles's indifference, had given up.

Eating his own modest breakfasts on the balcony after the war, with no solicitous parlourmaid to replenish the coffee or bring silver baskets of rolls under white napkins, Charles would often be reminded of those serene mornings, when his family created for him a happy and protected world. In the attempt at self-analysis in which he sometimes fashionably indulged, he would wonder whether in his dreams he was seeking to return to that repose, seeing in his sleep the quiet, sunlit garden and the finely ordered rooms of his childhood. Or was he nowadays merely using the house for his own, modern, purposes? Could he forget his parents, and live independently of them? Or did their spirits still inhabit the house and the garden, and indeed overshadow his own life? as sometimes on hot oppressive afternoons, when only the noise of the traffic violated the stillness, he believed.

Letter from Miss Barbara Gibbons to her friend Miss Sarah Wentworth

La Rosaille, Mentone,
Wednesday 7 April 1920

Dearest Sarah

I promised to write again soon and so here I go, boring you ON AND ON. I'm still having quite a nice time in Mentone, as everyone here calls it except the French who call it Menton (with a French accent) but I suppose we know better than them (than they? what would Miss Graham make us say?). My aunt and uncle are being very kind but it's a bit of a bore being with old people all the time though actually I have now made some ripping new friends at the tennis club. Anyway they seem ripping compared to the other people I've met and I'm all ready to have a GP on someone called Richard who is at Cambridge and his parents live here and he has quite long hair which he keeps throwing back from his forehead in rather a divine way and he likes medieval literature which is a bit off-putting but he's lovely in flannels so that makes up for it. His parents are quite the thing according to my uncle and aunt and they're keen to ask him to tea though tea is not what I have in mind. SAY NO MORE...

As you see I do chatter on which shows that I don't have anything very exciting to do here and miss you madly darling friend of my girlhood but at least I'm only here till the end of May when Everyone but Everyone leaves Mentone — I can't imagine how the town keeps going in those peculiar circs. I'm working hard on my French and you'd be amazed by the too too elegant way I employ the past subjunctive at the drop of a *chapeau*. Mademoiselle who teaches me French is very nice and we have quite a few giggles about my aunt and uncle — Cicely and Harry I call them but she's too polite.

Anyway the BIG EXCITEMENT is that after days of staying in we went to a lunch party on Easter Sunday!!! Quite a dizzy event here. C keeps asking me about my season last summer and I do my best to make it sound thrilling but giving a list of parties isn't very exciting especially since C doesn't know anyone and of course as we all know it was rather *piano* everyone being dead. From the way C and H went on you'd think we'd been asked to lunch by the Emperor of Japan. Because we were to meet an ecclesiastical GRANDEE we all went to Matins at the funny little English church here, actually there are two (and a Scottish one as well) but we went to the posh one. It's very ugly with a couple of droopy palm trees outside which look as though they'd joined the Church of England and found it a bit dispiriting. I was very nervous because before we went Cicely said to me, Barbara do be careful about what you say — there's been an unholy row (that's actually what she said, rather spirited of the old thing) about the vestry. The new vicar (who's considered a bit common by the old English and Scottish ladies, who are known as the 'aunts' here by the disrespectful) wanted to move the vestry from the room

on the right as you go into the church into the room on
the left, and move the library — which has the dullest
collection of books outside Wycombe Abbey — into the
room on the right. Or the other way round, I can't
remember. Apparently this decision has torn Mentone
COMPLETELY IN TWO!!! and caused terrible
unhappiness and half the English community isn't
speaking to the other half and lots of people won't go to
church because of the Evil Vicar's behaviour. Honestly
you would think he'd offered babies for sacrifice which
would certainly have livened things up though there aren't
any babies in Mentone. Anyway, said Auntie, DO BE
CAREFUL!!!! I was so nervous about saying something
like, Isn't it marvellous that the vestry is on the right
now? to some innocuous-looking old party and finding I
was talking to the left-hand vestry faction and becoming
a total PARIAH!!!! that I could hardly move. Too too
frightening! The thrill was that the Bishop of Gibraltar
no less was coming to the service. Who is the said
Bishop, I hear you ask. Well, he has charge of all the
English churches round the Mediterranean and further
and as far as I can see he waltzes around staying in nice
houses and being fussed over by pious ladies which
sounds nice if you're that kind of bishop. Anyway he
preached a sermon about loving kindness and loving your
neighbour, which went down like a Big Bertha at a
vicarage tea-party. He is quite nice but rather stout and
has no wife (and never had one, unless in some previous
undisclosed Life of Sin in Tasmania). What do you
think??? Shall I marry him and put an end to the
anxieties of my dear mother who is quite hysterical that

I'm now 19 and still not married and as we know too well nowadays there aren't as many chaps around as there were.

After the service Harry and Cicely and I looked very prim because WE were going to have lunch with the Bishop unlike everybody else. Cicely was quite naughty and as we were traipsing out ready to shake the hand of said bish she remarked to a vicious old woman called Miss Macpherson who lives only to say disagreeable things that she hoped Miss M would be celebrating Easter Day pleasantly – which of course led on to the information that we were Lunching With The Bishop. Miss M looked green and blue and we all relished her discomfiture though Harry pretended not to. As we reached the line to greet the Bishop C scored again and remarked that she mustn't keep his lordship long since we were seeing him at lunch. This she said loudly, infuriating the old trouts in the queue who looked DAGGERS!!!

Must stop since it's time for lunch here and now but I'll go on later. Hope I'm not boring you darling...

6 p.m.

Just able to snatch a moment after a semi-thrilling time at the tennis club – by the way how is your secretarial course don't take it too seriously – before changing for dinner though since I only have about one evening frock changing is an overstatement. Anyway since I know you're GRIPPED by my narrative I will go on about Easter Day. After routing all the old bags we went off to lunch. I'd heard about the Williamsons from C and H who say they're

quite the thing and her Sunday afternoon At Homes are
much enjoyed by the Mentone fashionable set (average age
106). Lovely place, big drive, large modern house (they're
all pretty modern, the houses people live in here, not the
houses in the Old Town which are Steeped in Antiquity
but nobody lives there) with balconies, lots of plants all
over the place, wisteria to die for over the verandah. When
we went into the house we were asked, TOO PECULIAR,
to wash our hands in a little washroom just inside the hall.
C and H said it was because Mrs W is terrified of disease
and dreads people bringing in germs. (Apparently once
when they returned a book she had lent them, she said,
Thank you very much and I will have it fumigated – C a
bit put out by this but then learnt this is her standard
practice.) I know you're interested in people's houses so
here goes. The hall – C says interior decoration is the
coming thing though what she knows about coming things
is nil – the hall is painted ivory I think you'd call it with a
big vaulted ceiling and a large mirror over the
chimneypiece and mostly English furniture but one or two
foreign-looking things, a big lacquer screen, all
old-fashioned but pretty. Then we were shown into the
drawing room by a Scottish lady who seemed to be the
governess or housekeeper or something, they were all very
easy with her. Drawing room had stripy wallpaper and
pale green curtains and some of those funny French
chairs, all gold and twisty, and a tapestry and sofas in the
English manner – goodness, French people's houses are SO
uncomfortable perhaps they never sit down always IN
BED getting up to Heaven Knows What. All the guests
are in the drawing room when I go in since I'm the last to

do the Great Wash so I feel shy. I'm the youngest by miles. Mrs Williamson is in a white dress with a blue bow, for Easter I suppose. She must be 45 or so, not thin but not fat though she needs to look out. Big brooch. She has a nice face not exactly pretty but smiley. She's very welcoming and says she's afraid I'll be bored with all these old people but if I come back as she hopes I will she'll find some young people for me to meet. Mr W is tall and sweet, in fact rather topping but looks anxious — he is rather pink in the face (from the sun and being so fair, not from drink I think) and looks sad when he's not talking but that must be the way his features lie. He introduces me to the Bishop again and I decide that even the possibility of life in the Bishop's Palace does not make it worth succumbing to the fumbling advances which he may make to me UNDER THE PALM TREES AS TWILIGHT FALLS, the gold cross on his purple chest becoming intimately linked with the buttons on my demure white blouse... SAY NO MORE ... Then he introduces me to a frightening couple called Mr and Mrs Hanson, who have a famous garden on Cap Martin. H and C practically die with excitement on being introduced and C says in the MOST EMBARRASSING WAY, 'Oh, we are so glad to make your acquaintance' (at least she doesn't say 'pleased to meet you') 'since we have heard so much about your beautiful gardens.' She says 'gardens' to make them sound more grand and curry favour with Mrs H who is very tall and patrician and organised-looking. Mrs H looks awfully bored and says, 'You must come and see them one day,' as enthusiastically as if C had offered to do a can-can on her lawn. C is not deterred and summons

H to tell him that Mrs Hanson has sweetly said they may see her gardens upon which Mrs H gives a frosty smile and asks me where I am at school. Not a good start and she can perfectly well tell I'm already out.

Then we all go in to lunch. The dining room is very pretty, pale grey walls with French curly decoration on the ceiling and a few watercolours, mostly English I'd say (don't you admire my genius as an observer?). The table looks wonderful with about six vases of flowers I can't begin to tell you what but they look DIVINE on the white tablecloth with huge table napkins and a big silver bowl in the middle full of fruit. Lots of knives and forks beside each place which looks promising since I have totally abandoned myself to food, you would be amazed to see how fat and jolly I have become no longer the slender goddess of yesteryear, also wine of which I drink as much as possible though H and C are hopeless on cocktails of which they've apparently never heard. H says he would never let gin into the house. Anyway I find myself between Uncle H and Mr Williamson. Mr W says to Aunt C in a debonair way, 'By rights you should be sitting here, Mrs Gibbons, but you see me often enough and we thought you would enjoy talking to Mr Hanson whom I don't think you've met before.' C is enchanted and she and Mr H who looks easier than his lady clearly have a good time, since C at least talks quite intelligently about plants. Bishop is next to Mrs Williamson of course and separated from me so I do not have to wonder whether I will feel the soft touch of a gaitered calf against my trembling leg, just as well probably since in the passion of the moment seduced by the lure of the Cloth I might have thrown myself at his feet (awkward to do in the dining room with all the chairs, not to speak of Mrs Hanson etc, it might have had to wait till the garden afterwards) and declared my undying love for the C of E and above all for him and Gibraltar where I pine to make my life. Mrs Hanson talks a lot to Mr Williamson about Italy. She says it was horribly disorganised after the war and the governments were hopeless and changed every five minutes and strong government was needed and this man Mussolini seems to have good ideas. Mr W mutters about the undervalued virtues of parliamentary democracy, but not very forcefully. Then they turn to gardens – nobody ever seems to have a serious conversation down here for more than about two minutes and you know what a serious-minded girl I am and long to talk about the impact of women's suffrage and why not the vote at twenty-one for us too. No chance of that. Meanwhile I try to look demure yet fetching and talk a bit to Uncle – he's stuck with Evil Vicar's Wife on his other side who looks like a submarine. I concentrate on lunch which is QUITE DELICIOUS and not at all like food at home. We have some wonderful spaghetti stuff – I think it's called knocky – filled with tomatoes and green slices, could they be peppers? which is so good that when we start eating it everyone falls silent for a moment until Mrs W rallies and asks the Bishop where he is bound for next. Then comes Chicken Marengo, which Napoleon invented in a railway carriage or something like that, and a delicious green vegetable dish called *plat vert*. I know one is not supposed to talk about food in POLITE SOCIETY unlike school so this is between ourselves. When I'm married to a marquess I shall have the most wonderful food like the Williamsons and talk about it all the time. The Williamsons' food is very rich and creamy and just the thing to celebrate Easter Day. No roast lamb thank goodness.

Oh God I mean oh Goodness I'm late for dinner that was the gong —

LATE AT NIGHT AFTER A THRILLING <u>DINER A TROIS</u> AND A HAND OF PIQUET WITH H — CAN I STAND THE PACE???

Back to the lunch. At last I have a chance to talk to Mr Williamson, he is perfectly CHARMING and I instantly transfer my passion from the Bishop to him. He asks all about me as though he's really interested and I tell him about school (not much, because the memory's so depressing apart from you and he doesn't want to hear about the cold or the callisthenics or what it was like getting the news about people's brothers being killed) — and the Season and about my parents. He's very interested to hear that Papa is so senior in the Home Office and tells me that he (Mr W) was in the Indian Civil Service until he had to leave because he had asthma. He asks me who I've met here and do I play tennis and would I like to play with him which I eagerly agree to, already planning an alluring costume though sadly he's married (it just shows what one's come to). I ask him whether the Bishop plays tennis and wears purple flannels and he laughs. So then I ask him what he most enjoys about living in the South of France (a subtle way of asking how he passes the time) and he says that he's setting up the Menton Players an amateur dramatic club and he's chairman and do I act? When I tell him I am leaving in July he looks quite sad and says, 'Never to return?' and I say in a sprightly way, 'No, my parents want me to look for a husband and I'm not sure this is the best place,' and then, very boldly (since he is so twinkly), 'I suppose the Bishop of Gibraltar doesn't need a wife?' at which he laughs quite loudly and his wife looks down the table rather surprised as though to say, What on earth are you laughing at? Meanwhile the pudding appears too too thrilling, it is called *riz à l'impératrice* and was created for the Empress Eugenie (not sure about the accents there and not sure who she was but apparently she used to live in Mentone until quite recently) by her brilliant chef and it is rice but cooked to taste sweet and full of candied fruit and honey and it is too utterly too. I have two helpings which the nice maid seems to find gratifying and Mr W is amused and begs me to have a third which I long to but it's a bit awkward since everyone is watching so I say No and he says Go on, it's a feast day, and I see Mrs W glowering a bit down the table so I say Yes and then have to eat it while everyone else has stopped, very embarrassing but fun. Mrs W looks awfully put out so I have to gobble – Really this letter is much too long but do tell me what you have been doing – I wonder if you and Celia are going to stay with the Forbeses...

Mentone is a quiet place that appears to take its pleasure demurely, if not sadly. It is marked too by a respectability which is commendable, but at the same time almost awe-inspiring. Perhaps its nearness to Monte Carlo makes this characteristic more prominent. If Monte Carlo be a town of scarlet silks, short skirts and high-heeled shoes Mentone is a town of alpaca and cotton gloves and of skirts so long that they almost hide the elastic-side boots.

There is a class of English lady – elderly, dour and unattached – that is comprised under the not unkindly term of 'aunt'. They are propriety personified. They are spoken of as 'worthy'. Although not personally attractive they are eminent by reason of their intimate knowledge of the economics of life abroad. To them those human mysteries, the keeper of the *pension*, the petty trader and the laundress are as an open book. They fill the frivolous bachelor with reverential alarm, but their acquaintance with the rate of exchange, the price of butter and the cheap shop is supreme in its intricacy. These 'aunts' are to be found in larger numbers in Mentone than in any other resort of the English in France.

SIR FREDERICK TREVES, BART., *The Riviera of the Corniche Road* (1921)

⊰ MARCH 1924 ⊱

R ECUMBENT AND HARDLY BORED, Mrs Williamson lay in bed one sunny morning and considered the advantages and disadvantages of her new *régime*, the *jour de repos*. Spending a day each week in bed, without disturbance or strain, was a custom she had lately adopted on medical advice. After ten weeks, she was considering whether she should continue.

Through the white curtains and half-drawn shutters she could see it was a fine day. If the warmth continued, she might step on to the balcony in the afternoon (that was allowed, she had ascertained) and benefit from the sunshine. But for the moment, while the air was still touched by morning coolness, she was safer in bed. Weekly rest was obviously advantageous to someone as delicate as herself, suffering from neuralgia as well as from the strain on her system of her days in India and the loss of her child. Happily, she was able to consult several doctors, especially Dr Campbell of Casa Rossa whom she particularly trusted and liked. (When they dined with the Campbells, as they did quite often, it was no embarrassment that he knew her so well, since he was so tactful, and his knowledge of plants was quite exceptional.) The doctor in Staffordshire, whom she saw in the summer, was also reliable, and sometimes she would call on specialist advice, in consultation, of course, with Dr Campbell. Dr Campbell was assiduous in visiting her at home, since for someone in her condition regular checks by a medical practitioner were essential. The doctors generally expressed their satisfaction with the care she took of herself and praised her sense in consulting doctors. Only occasionally would they tell her to take life more easily, a difficult course of action in view of her responsibilities, especially to Henry.

The doctors' support relieved the anxiety with which she had struggled for so long. And so did her house and, above all perhaps, her beautiful room, with its two great windows looking on to the sea. Her room – their room – was at last as she wanted it, the walls covered with the prettiest rather medieval-looking paper with a decoration of flowers and trellises from Cole's, and on the parquet floor three Oriental rugs, which were taken up if it became hot. The curtains were in pink silk from Lyons with, she thought, a handsome but not over-elaborate pelmet, all very much in the English style rather than the French (though of course she had not seen inside many French houses). She had kept the *cabinet de toilette*, like a little antechamber, which had been there when she arrived, and painted it ivory white. She thought that Edith Wharton would be pleased with her taste. And the furniture – the little pink velvet sofa, the dressing table in the Louis manner, the light but pretty tables which she and Henry had bought at Heal's just before the war, the single bookcase which contained her favourite books, created a comfortable but not at all oppressive room, she thought. Indeed, she was sure of it, since when she showed the room to her guests they always exclaimed with pleasure. Perhaps politeness obliged them to exclaim, but she thought their pleasure was genuine. Particularly important to her was the Chippendale chair with arms, just a single one they had found in a shop in Staffordshire when they were first married, since it was there that Henry sat when he was reading to her in the evening.

Was everything around her in order? She glanced at the bedside table, covered in the fresh white tablecloth which, as always, had been changed that morning by Emma. On it stood the bottle with the blue pills, without which she could not be properly at ease, the bottle with the red pills, and the smelling salts. A jug of lemonade with a little sugar (but not too much) and a glass awaited any intimation of thirst: it was always advisable to take as much fluid as possible. The drawer of the bedside table contained, in a discreet order known only to her and Emma, the medicines and private necessities essential to her health.

Below the bedside table stood another table, lower and movable. This was also reachable from the bed, though not very comfortably. This smaller table was used on the *jour de repos* or when she went to bed early. It supported a small library, since there was no objection to her reading anything she liked. Today it held a new novel in the Tauchnitz edition called *The Enchanted April*, by the mysterious author of that delightful book *Elizabeth and her German Garden*. This seemed to be about sad repressed Englishwomen being liberated from the gloom of England and finding a new happiness in a castle in Italy, beside the water. Ah, well, she thought, that was a happy idea. Beside it lay a favourite older book of hers on Venetian society in the eighteenth century, accompanied (for more serious reading) by that difficult-looking book *The Decline of the West* by a German writer called Spengler, which

Henry was always pressing upon her (he had made extensive notes in the margins). Together these would keep her entertained and interested: variety and stimulus in literature were good for her, unlike variety and stimulus in her diet. On the other hand, she needed to spend two hours in the afternoon lying with eyes closed and if possible asleep (though not too heavily asleep, since this might not be healthy and might prevent her sleeping at night).

Comfortably walled around by the apparatus of domesticity and medical care, she lay gravely, her auburn hair stretching luxuriantly over the white covers.

On the subject of Henry's health, the doctors were also most useful. Henry, she had found, was not at all anxious to see doctors even every week or two weeks. When she suggested a visit to the doctor, just to see how he was, he would say crossly – or as crossly as he ever did – that he felt perfectly well. Of course she was pleased and would not disabuse him if he thought so. But it was her mission to care for him and check that he never became too hot or cold, since maintaining a regular temperature was vital for someone with pulmonary disorders. So when he went into the garden she would ensure in spring that he always wore a hat, and that his clothes were pleasantly light but able to cope with the changes of temperature or occasional burst of rain that afflicted even Mentone's almost perfect climate. In winter she would insist that he wore at least a sleeveless jersey under his jacket – though he said he hated wearing too many clothes – to maintain a steady body heat. On one occasion recently she had seen him leaving the house in December in nothing but shirt sleeves – yes, in December (although it was quite a mild winter, there was always a cool undercurrent in the air). She had had to rush after him with his jersey. He seemed vexed rather than grateful: this had shocked her and she had almost wept. She had protested, 'But, Henry, I only do it for your good, you must be sensible or what will become of you? I can't let you stroll around in midwinter wearing nothing but a shirt.' All he replied was, 'Oh, very well, I'll wear an overcoat at all times, like a prisoner's outfit, even in summer.' When she pleaded with him to be reasonable and not sarcastic he subsided into, 'Very well, Helen, very well. Whatever you want shall be done.' That had not been altogether nice, either. So it was reassuring to be told by the doctors that he must indeed take care, or the asthma might resume, and that changes of temperature and too much exercise and even such things as working in the garden all offered dangers.

She wondered whether to drink some lemonade but was discouraged by the effort of locating glass and jug. This was perhaps rather lazy of her, but on her *jour de repos* it was surely good for her to be lazy – wasn't that the point of the *régime*? Instead she admired the look of her fine white hand – so English in its whiteness, she thought, so unlike those of Frenchwomen, particularly in this part of the world, who could never achieve such purity. She studied it against the strong clarity of the tone of the linen sheet. The light that entered the room from the half-closed shutters was beginning to shift towards her face and she might have to ring for Emma to adjust the shutter, though usually Emma would come in about now. The soft cream of her bed dress (into which she had changed that morning, it would not do to remain in the clothes she had worn during the night) showed with particular richness against the sheets, and she felt that the blue ribbon that threaded through the smocking and which she had chosen after much discussion with Emma added an appropriate accent.

Ah, but this was absurd, she told herself, it was not as though she were being painted, and there was nobody there to see her or to admire the contrasts in colour. Charles might have done perhaps, although perhaps not, but Charles was away at school. He was not enthusiastic about visiting his mother in her bedroom, and had made a great fuss about reading to her one evening during the previous holidays when Henry had a sore throat.

But nobody else was unhelpful. She was so fortunate that dear Betty ran the house so smoothly, not always easy with four servants indoors and two gardeners plus the chauffeur, and so much entertaining and the two boys during the holidays and quite a number of visitors from England, some of whom would stay for a month or so. Of course, she herself kept an eye on everything and planned the menus with the cook. This was taxing, since she had to remember everything that she and Henry should not eat, and make sure that visitors were never given the same dish twice running, and that the diet was properly balanced. Betty, of course, ensured that the accounts were in order, but she always checked them. And she spent a lot of time on organising the entertaining they all enjoyed, even though Henry sometimes said things like, 'Oh, another lunch party, must we?' or even 'Do we have to have that woman to lunch again? She has no conversation and isn't even nice to look at.' There was always the worry that she might need to make a private visit during a meal, which was, of course, so difficult in other houses though in one's own one could manage it under the guise of seeing all was well in the kitchen or attending to the flowers. As for the garden — well, that took a great deal of her time, reliable though Franco was, and she was constantly having to supervise the planting and the care of the plants.

So with all this strain, there emerged — she forgot who had the idea, was it she herself, or Dr Campbell? — the *jour de repos*. No distractions or telephone calls (unless she had to ring somebody urgently, as was often essential). Total rest. Emma brought her the regular meals she must eat to sustain her strength. There had been some difficulty over finding a suitable bed-tray but the Army and Navy Stores had solved that problem, like so many.

Through her windows she could see the tops of the palm trees, and the shining sea in the distance. Confined though she was, and denied everyday pleasures, she found these *jours de repos* not unpleasant, the solitude punctuated by meals, which it was her duty to consume, and Henry's visits, and her maid's attentions. With Henry she would discuss Italian Renaissance art and architecture (those books by Mr Bernard Berenson were extremely interesting, particularly when one had seen so many of the museums and palaces) and the history of Venice. And there was reassurance in the thought that though she spent the days mostly alone she could, by touching the bell, summon all the society the house offered.

Emma entered, carrying a vase of white irises for the round table in the middle of the room, and a little pile of letters, which she placed on the larger bedside table, with a paper knife. How lucky she was to have Emma to look after her, so devoted, so efficient, so quiet, her own age and really a friend rather than a servant. Except in the summer, when she went to Switzerland to see her family, Emma was always there to look after her, to assist with her various medical needs, to supervise her clothes, making sure that they always looked as they should and altering them discreetly when necessary, to advise on new clothes and often make them, to lay out her day clothes, to help her into a tea gown when that was needed, to help select the dress for the evening when she changed, above all to assist her when she was preparing for a luncheon engagement. Emma took such pride . . .

'Will you close the shutters?' she was going to ask, but Emma was already moving towards the window, looking towards the bed to see how far the sunlight had reached: already the bars of the window frames were making shadows on the counterpane. Emma opened the heavy windows, and closed the great green shutters against the sun. Sunlight was so cruel, and she was sure it was bad for the complexion. Then the maid came towards the bed, enquiring whether she was feeling rested, and if it would be convenient to bring lunch at one. Without being asked, she poured out a glass of lemonade and handed it to Helen. Gratefully she took it, recalling how Aunt Susan had looked after her as a child when she was ill – quite a frequent occurrence, even then. Lunch at one would be fine, since she felt in need of a proper afternoon rest, and yes, a glass of wine would probably be restorative. She let Emma plump up her pillows and look around the bed and its surroundings to ensure all was in perfect order.

Everybody was so kind, she thought, and understanding. On these special days, the servants moved around the house even more gently than usual, under Betty's supervision. Wednesday was the usual *jour de repos*, and it was unusual for anyone to call then since Mrs Williamson's day of rest was already recognised in a quiet, respectful way throughout the British community. So in bed she would lie all day, comfortably incarcerated in her pink and white bedroom beneath the cages of flowers.

She considered the pile of letters beside her bed. There was one from her sister-in-law in England, asking when they would be coming over in the summer and whether they were going to Italy this year. Her old schoolfriend Ethel wrote, with an amusing drawing of a picnic and the picnic party being attacked by a bull. And there was a letter from Charles at Eton, which she had opened with less enthusiasm.

In her happy life, with the fine sense of home that she had created, the perfectly ordered house surrounded by a garden that each year seemed closer to Paradise, Charles was the only disturbance. Perhaps that was too hard a word. He was sixteen now, and getting to be difficult, though his reports suggested that he was exceptionally gifted. 'A talented and interesting boy, who has read far more than most of his contemporaries or even than those much older than himself.' ... 'This very clever boy shows considerable promise. I am startled to discover not only that he is teaching himself Italian, but that he reads Dante in the original, rather than the Binyon translation most of us use!' ... 'His knowledge of Latin and Greek and the ease with which he grasps subtle points in their development is remarkable in one of his years.' ... His tutor was already raising the question of which university he would be sent to – no doubt it would be Oxford, where Henry had gone, and probably his old college. His tutor also wrote of Charles's enthusiasm for writing, though it was not perhaps the most profitable activity for him, particularly if he was intended for the diplomatic service. She hoped so much that he would have a brilliant career in the public service, and the Foreign Office did seem the most suitable: it was so distinguished, and he would be able to travel, and she was sure that his writing abilities would be fulfilled there.

But, clever as he was, he was undoubtedly difficult. Henry, who was particularly attached to Charles, would not admit it. There had been an unhappy moment during the previous holidays, one she never forgot. It recurred to her in the last days of her life when in the hectic and frightened moments that intruded into their cool, careful planning she remembered how her life had passed. One day she had complained of not feeling well, of a pain in her side. Henry was expressing anxiety, when Charles abruptly exclaimed, 'M'tutor says the health of the mind and the body are intimately linked. Lots of people think their bodies are ill when actually it's their minds. They're depressed or worse. If they were happier or more balanced they wouldn't be ill.' She remembered these words too well; why did she need to remember them? There had been a silence and Henry had then spoken, too hesitantly she thought. That was an interesting theory, he said, but of course many people had deep-seated physical problems for which such explanations could not be valid. To which Charles had scornfully answered, 'Some people are just ill because they don't have anything better to do. And they make everyone else run round and look after them, if they're lucky enough to have people to do it and the other people are stupid enough to agree.' There had been another silence and then Betty asked Henry whether he was going to Nice during the next few days because she needed some things collected, and Francis had observed, blushing, that he wanted to play tennis that afternoon and he hoped the Knoxes would be there because the girls were such fun and he wondered if Ma would ask them to lunch one day since she knew their mother who was awfully nice too. Which, strengthened by the look of support and love in his eyes, she gladly agreed to.

Nobody discussed the episode. She wondered whether Henry would mention it, but when he came to read to her that evening he only looked at her, as she thought enquiringly, and opened the volume of memoirs of the court of Louis XIV which he was reading to her at the time.

She did not know why she was upset, or why she remembered the episode. Nothing Charles said applied to her. She was not ill by choice, nor unhappy; on the contrary she lived in the most contented of households, with the best of husbands, and had no worries except for others. And it seemed an absurd theory, too, since as Henry said some people were simply cursed with ill health. But the way that Charles had spoken had been so fierce that for all her powers of reason she had felt under attack. Why could her son not realise that though she tried to be as good a mother as she could, she needed to be looked after herself? Charles's approach was so unlike that of her darling Francis, with whom everything was easy and happy, and who never questioned her or did anything to disturb the ease and grace of their life together.

Feverish at the recollection of her son's darkened face, she considered his letter more carefully. It was unexceptionable:

dutiful, amusing and affectionate. He told his parents about the effect of light on the Thames in the early summer evenings, and how he had been studying the plants in Luxmoore's Garden and found the choice of planting on the whole rather banal in spite of the general praise for it. And he sent many kind messages to his mother, and hoped she was feeling better with the spring weather . . .

In the midst of these thoughts Emma re-entered. She took the bed-tray from its place beside the cupboard and stood it on the bed so that Helen, leaning against her pillows, could eat comfortably. Then she went out of the room and returned carrying the customary lacquer tray, the traycloth decorated with blue embroidered flowers, something she had sewn herself in her youth. Upon the tray was a little helping of *oeufs aux tomates*, a Spanish dish, which though spicy was easy to digest. Under a silver cover, there lay, Helen knew (having given the menu some thought the previous day), a helping — more generous than she could manage — of the *soufflé au poisson Nantua* which she found particularly delicious when well. Shall I put the soufflé on the side table? asked Emma, but no, that would not be necessary. But the glass of wine — white, and again, larger than she could probably manage to drink, she would only take a mouthful — was placed on the table, as were the glass of water and the vase of narcissi that adorned the tray. The bread roll with its accompanying butter shell could, she thought, remain on the tray, but the dish of fruit salad was happier on the table. Does Madame have everything she needs? asked Emma. Yes, she did, she replied, arranging the napkin around her neck and hoping Emma would go soon since she preferred to take her lunch unobserved. She eyed the eggs, which must not be allowed to get cold since they would congeal, while the soufflé could be left for ten minutes or so . . .

She did not disenjoy her lunch although she was not able to finish it, leaving a spoonful or two of the *oeufs aux tomates*. The wine she did drink, considering it would not hurt her and might help her to doze in the afternoon. And when the tray had been removed, the shutters fully closed and the pillows rearranged once again, she was able to rest at last.

Old Mentone dreams in the sombre shadows of its doorways. Young Mentone basks in the sunshine of the Promenade du Midi.

Old Mentone climbs with clattering sabots over the rough cobble-stones of her narrow, centuries-old streets. Young Mentone swings along in tennis shoes or whirls past in shining automobiles . . .

Young Mentone hears the town news over a bridge table, sends her maître d'hôtel to market, and threads her dainty way among the nurse-maids and governesses in the Jardin Publique, or saunters along the sunny promenade bestowing a sweet but perfectly impersonal word here and there.

And all that Old Mentone knows of Young Mentone is that at certain times of the year she comes with her governesses, her babies, her luggage and her benefit-of-exchange, to live in the big hotels and villas which are a terra incognita to her neighbour.

And all that Young Mentone knows of Old Mentone is that she lives in dark, smelly streets, speaks an unintelligible patois, and only appears on the Promenade du Midi on Sunday afternoons when she herself leaves it generously free that one day in the week.

YSABEL DE WITTE, *The Romance and Legend of the Riviera*

A FTER BREAKFAST, which was solitary, and after
reading *The Times* of three days ago which had just
arrived, walking round the garden (without putting on a
jacket, since Helen was in bed and could not supervise his
wardrobe) and admiring the ducks on the long pond, Henry
felt it was time to go to his room. This was his bedroom, on
the second floor, where he generally slept, but it also
contained his desk and his papers and his favourite books.
He reflected as he went into the room that many of these
were books about British and classical history, and India,
which he had read in his youth or while in the Indian Civil
Service. Now he hardly looked at them. Perhaps he should
throw them away or give them away or at least move them to
one of the many ample bookcases in the passages. Not yet
awhile, though.

Henry sat down at his desk and considered what he
ought to do. There was a meeting of the committee of the
Lawn Tennis and Croquet Club of Mentone next week. He
would be presiding, and the papers lay on his desk. Not
many problems here. The club was respectably in the black,
and had more applications for membership than it could
accept. It was surprising how many English and other
foreign people were nowadays coming to Mentone in the
summer for holidays, and even staying through the horribly

hot months of July and August — as the survivors of the traditional English community, invalids in search of health, believed them to be. Ten years ago, nobody had stayed in the summer. Many of these new visitors were young and active and not particularly interested in the health-giving qualities of Mentone, so that the town had changed from being the outdoor sanatorium of their early days there into a holiday resort. No more threat of malaria, that was the reason. He wondered sometimes whether the town had ever had health-giving qualities. Recalling all those premature deaths among the foreign community in the early years of the century, he doubted it.

Mentone remained quiet, its hill crowned by its cemetery, not at all like the more dashing towns to the west. To these they hardly ever went: though they might venture to Monte Carlo and Nice, they never journeyed as far as Cannes. He and Helen were hardly affected by the changes along the coast, leading the quiet life they preferred at home and returning to England every summer. But they were pleased to be reminded of home, as they still called England. So, if temporary visitors from Britain wanted to join the Lawn Tennis and Croquet Club for a month or two they were heartily welcomed by Henry, even though some members disliked the interruption of their routine by temporary residents.

Otherwise the meeting held no problems. A report on new members, and the waiting list. The death of an old member, whom he could hardly remember — would a minute of silence be appropriate or was that reserved only for defunct committee members? At least a silence would liven up the meeting. A report from the new professional coach from England, a helpful and co-operative young man. A report on the maintenance of the grounds. The question of extending the service of tea to members, on Thursdays and Fridays only, up to five o'clock instead of half past four, as at present. This was a tricky issue, to be delegated to a sub-committee. He was all in favour himself, but radical changes of this sort were viewed with suspicion by members and by the secretary, for whom it might create additional work. Such an innovation would cause mayhem at the AGM. ('Mayhem at the AGM' – a title for a skit for the Menton Players?) The appointment of a new honorary secretary, to succeed Colonel Hughes, who was finding the duties too strenuous. There was no shortage of applicants: membership of the committee was seen as an honour, putting one at the heart of the British community.

Under the papers for the Lawn Tennis and Croquet Club lay the papers for the Menton Players. This amateur dramatic society had been founded before the Great War, had languished, had been revived by Henry among others, and now offered one of the principal amusements for expatriates. It performed in the handsome auditorium of the Grand Casino, which was well equipped and could manage plays of reasonable size. Gilbert and Sullivan had been found demanding because of the size of the cast (though musical expertise was high) and Shakespeare severely tested elocution and interpretation, but plays by Pinero and Somerset Maugham (whom the 'aunts' sometimes found rather strong) and Noël Coward and A. P. Herbert were presented to enthusiastic audiences. Henry enjoyed his involvement as producer, stage manager and performer. The dramas back-stage, which were numerous and tempestuous, were less enjoyable, but could be subdued with patience.

A handful of letters lay on his desk, where he had thrown them after breakfast. He scanned the envelopes. A letter from his brother Richard, always informative if not amusing. A communication from his bank. A letter from San Remo, addressed to the President of the Lawn Tennis Club, no doubt an application for membership or a complaint from one of the members who found complaint one of life's major pleasures.

Under these lay a letter labelled in familiar capital letters 'ON HIS MAJESTY'S SERVICE' and postmarked 'LONDON SW'.

What could this be?

To control irrational curiosity, he opened the other letters first. All were as predicted. Richard reported that business at the law firm was brisk, his wife was blossoming and so was her herbaceous border, the children were enjoying life at school (why did parents harbour these fantasies? he wondered). The bank had nothing of interest to report: everything seemed all right (or, as the American phrase had it, 'OK'.) The applicant for membership from San Remo had a double-barrelled name and a minor title and would certainly be acceptable to the sternest member of the application committee, possibly being allowed to vault over the waiting list though Henry disapproved of this.

The last letter was from an old acquaintance at the India Office, a man with whom for some years he had exchanged little more than routinely seasonal communications. Prefaced by many disclaimers and apologies, in which he recognised a familiar tone of confident authority, it informed him that the Office was commissioning a report on an important matter of administration (not specified) in India. An assessor outside the service but with some experience of its workings was sought to guide its deliberations. While, the letter acknowledged, Henry had left the service quite a number of years before, it was considered that in view of his distinguished achievement while in post and his knowledge of India, he would be a suitable person for such a position ... a journey to London for discussion would be necessary in the fairly near future ... only six to eight months ... two or three visits to London to attend meetings ... all expenses met and an honorarium ...

On finishing the letter, Henry did not move for some time. He glanced at the papers for the next meeting of the Menton Players. He looked at the flowered linen curtains around the windows, which Helen thought suitable. He considered his single bed and the convenient reading lamp on the night table. On either side of the fireplace squatted an armchair. One, in rich brown leather, was for him; the other was for a visitor (though few penetrated this sanctum). Each chair was accompanied by a little table, for glasses of whisky and soda or whatever. Helen, who had planned much of the room, considered the consumption of manly drinks suitable for such an apartment, though smoking was perhaps going too far. On two sides of the room towered large mahogany bookcases, crammed with volumes neatly arranged (and catalogued in notebooks) by their owner. There were two watercolours by Romilly Fedden, who had just visited the house. And watercolours by Alfred East and Alfred Hayward and other artists, which Henry had found on visits to London.

He was fond of the room. It communicated directly

with Helen's bedroom. It enjoyed magnificent views of the ambiguously smiling Mediterranean, which offered so little activity for the observer, and across which no great ship ever sailed that they could see, only sportive yachts and hard-working fishing-boats.

He must consider a few books that could be read to Helen, since they were almost at the end of *Crome Yellow*. What should he propose – since these decisions were always made jointly? Strachey's *Life of Queen Victoria*? H. G. Wells's *Short History of the World* (short though it might call itself, still perhaps rather long)? Should they revisit Henry James – though he was so difficult to read aloud? Edith Wharton, perhaps *The Age of Innocence*? Or should they address Shakespeare's sonnets, which they had always meant to read straight through?

It was time to go downstairs and prepare for his visit to the tennis club: he was due to play before lunch, and must speak to the honorary secretary, who was on duty from ten to twelve. He made for the door. Then he turned, found the letter from Whitehall, folded it into his pocket, and left again.

☙ RECOLLECTIONS ❧

A FTER THE SECOND WORLD WAR, Charles would often walk or drive down the avenue Carnot in Mentone on one of the errands that took much of his time in the early days of repairing the house. The avenue Carnot was the site of the Lawn Tennis and Croquet Club, but no club stood there any longer. Its terrain had been swallowed during the occupation by Italian soldiers, who must have enjoyed destroying the soft green evidence of British affection for sport and nature. Probably they were the same soldiers who threw the statue of Queen Victoria into the sea. After the war the club had been resurrected but the old site had been sold for redevelopment.

There was no vestige now of the old building. No trace of the discreet notice intended for tradesmen (since any member or guest would know where to go), of the ambitious stone gate piers erected in memory of Mr C. Thompson OBE, for many years honorary secretary, by his family and friends, of the two-storey clubhouse with its verandah (very like India, people used to say), of the lovingly protected and watered lawns. Inside the clubhouse there had been a card and smoking room for gentlemen only, a lounge and tea-room, a bridge room, and a room where light lunches and teas prepared in the English manner were served. The style of decoration was solid and altogether like home, rather darker than was becoming fashionable elsewhere but all the more reassuring for that. The walls boasted a very large portrait in oils of Queen Victoria, presented by Miss Scott to commemorate the Diamond Jubilee: the Queen was believed to have visited the clubhouse's predecessor during her memorable Mentone stay in 1882. Rather smaller images (not in oils) portrayed her son and grandson. There were lists of members and painted boards commemorating winners of the major cups. Not a word of French, other than proper names, appeared on any of the notices that busily announced club activities.

Visits to the club had always gained parental approval during Charles's youth. It offered, after all, healthy exercise, suitable if not always exciting people, opportunities to make new friends, and not least a reasonable sprinkling of young girls of the sort a young man would be happy to invite home. He and his brother spent a great deal of time there, playing tennis hour after hour, chatting to their friends the Knoxes, drinking tea and occasional cocktails. It was at least more amusing than some of the other prescribed entertainments – and was Mentone not famous for being the dullest town along the Riviera, much less fun than Monte Carlo or even Nice? (As A. P. Herbert put it, so far as Charles remembered, 'If you think Mentone is dull, Try a wet Sunday in Hull.') The Victoria Park Tea-rooms, for example – who in their right mind, Charles wondered, would choose to go there? These tea-rooms, close to the English Church of St John, were regarded by the 'aunts' as infinitely superior to any French equivalent. French bars were beyond all bounds, potentially immoral (though that was seldom actually said) and served horrid foreign drinks, too sweet or too bitter and not at all the thing. 'How could anyone like vermouth?' the English ladies would ask one another, not that they had tried it themselves, of course. Even the cafés, modest establishments on the whole, where the unassuming French *dames* of Mentone would gather of an afternoon, were not considered suitable or pleasant. They were so hot and ill-aired, and full of French people – not that one disliked the French but the ones down here were rather, well, ordinary, weren't they? And, of course, the proprietors had no idea at all of how to make tea, simply dropping a tea-bag (what an appalling invention, the tea-bag, with no resemblance at all to real tea) into tepid water with dreary results, and no understanding at all that one must use hot water and pour it straight on to the leaves. And French cakes, covered in cream and odd flavourings, were not at all nice (young friends from England sometimes displayed a heedless appetite for them and had to be warned off), much too rich and not to be compared with the fare at the Victoria Park Tea-rooms. There, the proprietors (who, though they appeared as genteel as could be, were reputed to have started their careers in the service of the Duchess of Sutherland and to have accompanied her to Mentone in that capacity) made the most excellent English cakes, sponge and chocolate, and Bakewell tart, and certainly knew how to make a good pot of tea. Above all, only the nicest sort of person was seen there – or, if not necessarily nice in the sense of someone one wished to spend one's time with, at least well-bred. On most days, one could go in there and feel quite at home, knowing absolutely everyone, if not personally at least by sight. A pleasant feeling it was, living in a foreign country, to feel so much at home even if one was not on good terms with everyone . . .

Oh, God, said Charles to himself, contemplating the more Bohemian lives of the English colony he knew in Mentone twenty-five years later, had it really been like that? And why had his father and mother interred themselves in such a society?

Worse than the Victoria Park Tea-rooms, with their photographs of English seaside resorts and their slightly modified Victorian décor, were the *thés dansants*. These were organised in great numbers all over the town – he recalled without enthusiasm the conversations at lunch when his mother nagged him to attend – at the Casino, the Imperial, the Astoria, the Royal Westminster, the Winter Palace. Nobody went out in the evenings, except to the rare performances of the Menton Players, so that afternoon dancing gained allure for the young. What young, exactly? Himself and his brother, when home from school or university, a few other boys in the same position, one or two girls staying with their parents. The girls tended to outnumber the boys (who generally hated attending these gatherings), and would be wheeled round the floor by their fathers in some shaming version of a no-longer-quite-fashionable dance or, not quite so bad, would dance something which had gone out ten years before but at least could later be imitated derisively at parties in England. There was a small unfortunate band, which gave the impression that its players had been unable to find any other employment or were unfrocked priests, strong on smiles, short on rhythm. Fruit cup was available, as well as tea. The fruit cup was supposed to be slightly alcoholic, but however much one drank, it made no impression. And there was tea and cakes, and lots of sitting out, and gossip, and as the tea began to bite, some coy dancing by the older ladies. It was true that his brother Francis and some of his friends seemed to enjoy these outings a great deal and that Francis sometimes went every day with his latest flame, but Charles never saw any point in them.

Then there was the society provided by the tennis club. His father, good-natured, urbane, intelligent (as Charles saw him in retrospect, the old contempt healed by time), had for twenty years presided over this organisation. What had made him give so much energy and attention to its affairs? The tennis club, apart from providing recreation for a few expatriates, contributed nothing to society but apparently considered that society was defined by its activities. Empires might totter (and did); the British Empire itself looked threatened; Italy might grow menacing under dictatorship, even though it was surely alien to the Italian character; the unemployed might march from Jarrow; Wall Street might collapse; Germany might become monstrous. But the Lawn Tennis and Croquet Club of Mentone rolled on. There, the greatest conflicts were waged between the supporters of Mrs Pattison and Mrs Loader for the chairmanship of the Ladies' Group, or between camps divided over the choice of striped or plain deck-chairs, or between the indisputably genteel and the indisputably rich (whose offers to pay for improvements were received coolly by those who could not have paid themselves). At least there were no nationalist disagreements, other than a few good-humoured border disputes between English and Scots. On the other hand, hardly any French people belonged, and those who did generally had English spouses or at least cousins. If French was overheard on the verandah, it would incite not overt curiosity or disapproval (which would be rude) but a puckered lip or raised eyebrow, faint but to other initiates perceptible. Someone had once suggested to Charles that in such places as the tennis club the way of life of the British community in India had been revived, with the French in the unfortunate role of the subordinate native population.

Charles's mother gave up tennis quite early and never again touched a racquet. But Pa went on playing, dancing around the court: he was considered an entertaining though unaccomplished player. The club was an important element of life, though he often joked about the tedium of the conversation. It reminded him, he used to say, of India, the attentive servants, the clubhouse surrounded by a verandah on which the members would sit watching the game or snoozing, the brilliant weather, the transposed Englishness of it all. Not that he regretted India, of course.

God, Charles would say to himself, how could I have stood it for five minutes, this mediocre limited life? . . . Had the place not affected his parents, shrinking their horizons? Had his mother's sense of isolation not been exacerbated by this claustrophobic atmosphere?

When the rebuilding of the tennis club site was taking place, he more than once took a walk along the avenue Carnot, to witness the demolition. It gave him a sense of release, surprising perhaps in a man dedicated to the pursuit and creation of beauty.

⇥ MARCH 1924 ⇤

T WO DAYS AFTER the letter from Whitehall had
arrived, Henry raised the matter. They were sitting in
the *petit salon* after dinner with Betty Gordon. Somewhat
diffidently (though why should she be diffident, Henry
wondered, after so many years?) Betty had asked when they
would be moving to England this year, and whether they
would be going to Italy first. The thought of this upheaval
always induced anxiety in Helen, who liked to stay in a place
once settled there, but it was, of course, essential. They were
leaving in early May, they said, and going to Venice for a
fortnight. Would Betty be coming with them?

Betty thought not. She would of course rejoin them in
Staffordshire, but there had been various events in her
family, and a wedding was impending...

'We always miss you, Betty,' said Henry, with his smile,
staring meanwhile at the table on which lay a complicated
solitaire. 'Life is so disorganised without you. All my fault, of
course, Helen manages beautifully but I'm quite hopeless.'

'Betty, of course you must go,' said Helen. 'We can
manage one way or another. But we shall need you in
Staffordshire and perhaps you could arrive a day or two
before us. It's so depressing when we go back, now that Aunt
Susan's no longer there.' And then, recollecting herself, 'If
necessary, we'll stay longer in Venice and perhaps go to

Florence on the way, to give you more time. We must do our best to keep Betty happy, Henry, or she will find a position in an aristocratic household, won't you, Betty, with a yacht and dozens of servants, dancing every night and cocktails by the pint, altogether much more amusing a situation than living with this quiet little family in a corner of the Riviera?'

'It's possible,' she replied. 'As you know the offers are frequent and proposals from a duchess and especially a Scottish duchess are not to be trifled with.'

'From a duchess, indeed? Not that naughty Duchess of Sutherland?' Helen answered, laughing. Conversations of this sort were common between them. 'Ah, Betty, life without you would be insupportable. I should die if you left us, Betty.'

This was a frequent lament, or threat, on the part of Helen. It was generally received with a smile and without comment.

On this characteristic evening of comfortable monotony, Miss Gordon used the occasion of Helen's plaint to fold up her sewing and make ready to depart, remarking, as she quite often did, out of habit and in mild reproach, 'And how is progress on the tapestry cover?' Helen had for some years been embroidering a tapestry cover for one of their eighteenth-century French chairs. She and Henry had bought the chairs at the end of the Great War in a little town in the Haute Savoie, encouraged by the story that they had come from a nearby château and had been confiscated during the Revolution. The seat cover was now complete but the back was taking some time.

'Ah,' said Helen vaguely, 'I think I'm making progress.'

'There's a sweepstake, you know, darling,' remarked her

husband, 'that you won't complete the chair before 1930. I believe it's arousing a lot of interest in Monte Carlo and that the Prince himself is taking a key part.'

'I don't have enough time, Henry,' she answered. 'Good night, Betty. Is anything happening tomorrow?'

No, nothing. And Betty, who tended to disappear early in the evenings, partly out of consideration for her employers and partly because she had no other time of the day to herself, departed.

(Did Betty have a life of her own? Charles would wonder in later years, when he recalled his childhood. She never appeared to see her own friends outside Scotland or to have days off. She had been the most amusing and kind governess any child could hope for, always ready with a new idea to entertain and instruct her charges, always firm, always aware of the moment when teaching could be pushed no further. 'Oh, give me patience,' she would cry, when her charges became too exuberant. But whether she had any private life, any emotional life, as it would now be known, whether she was ever in love, he did not know. Could she have been in love with his father? No, surely not. Had she ever lost her heart to one of those wounded officers during the war? Were her feelings dedicated to the whole family, to which she gave her best years, almost three decades? None of this anyone could know.)

When she had gone, Henry put down his cards and told his wife about the letter. She sat in silence for a moment, then asked, 'And what do you wish to do?'

'I wanted to ask you,' he replied.

'Would it be interesting, lovey darling?' she asked.

He thought it might be interesting. And perhaps some

of the work would be undertaken in the summer, when they were generally in England anyway.

Yes, that was a consideration.

There was a pause.

'Do you think you are strong enough?' she wondered. 'It would be taxing, I suppose. Meetings, travel, all those papers. But if you want to do it, darling, of course you must. Though I think you should speak to Dr Campbell about it all.'

Henry, back with his solitaire, laid down another card. Was this discouragement? No. Was this sensible caution? Well, perhaps. Why had he been tempted to say yes for a moment or two in the morning brightness? Vanity? Boredom? A wish to involve himself again in public affairs, which he really disliked? Would such work lead to more work, would he become over-involved?

'I doubt I'll take it,' he said, placing a king on his pile of hearts and smiling at his success – this solitaire was so difficult.

'You must not refuse it for my sake,' she answered.

A log fell out of the fire, missing the fireguard, and he hurried to catch it before it rolled on to the carpet.

'Our routine, our life here, is so important,' he said. 'You have created such a wonderful home for us all. I wouldn't want to disturb it.'

'Oh Henry,' she said, glowing. Had she been nimbler she would have caught and embraced him. Realising in a half-second that she could hardly achieve this, she raised her right arm and waved it at him.

Since Helen generally went to bed so early, sometimes before dinner, Henry was in the custom of spending an hour or so in his room, reading, before he went to bed himself. That night he did not read. He found on the shelves three or four of the essential books on India, which he had used as a young man, and dropped them into the wastepaper basket. He did not throw them, or hurl them, or even use any particular force in letting them go. He simply dropped them. He knew that nobody would question whether the contents of the basket were to be disposed of. In the morning it was taken away. So, to the post, was his letter to Whitehall, declining the offer, with many thanks for their kindness in thinking of him as a possible candidate.

⊱ APRIL 1946 ⊰

CHARLES CAME BACK to the empty house in the spring of 1946. It had not been easy to obtain official permission to travel or export money for the journey and living expenses, but he had pleaded with the authorities to be allowed to revisit his family property. With some difficulty he had gained the right to travel and to take twenty-five pounds out of the country.

He travelled to Mentone on the train that left Calais in the afternoon and stopped in Paris for a few hours, obliging travellers either to remain in the train as it undertook a mysterious loop journey from the Gare du Nord to the Gare de Lyons, or allowing them to leave the train for a few hours and have dinner (if it could be afforded) in the city. Charles, who had secreted some additional pound notes on his person, had looked forward for weeks to his first French meal since before the war. He paid homage to the Tuileries Gardens, looked at the river, breathed the distinctive Métro smell, and spent some of his francs on a dinner which, although it was not as delicious as the restaurant meals of his childhood, offered a spare richness of flavour he had not experienced for years. He sat up all night in the train, sharing the compartment with five or sometimes seven other people. He hardly slept, reliving boyhood journeys home from school, alone or with Francis. On these occasions he had been allowed a couchette and given money for dinner — a real treat — in the restaurant car. No such comfort today. What had not changed was the excitement of arrival on the Côte d'Azur, waking from the dismal slumber that had overcome him around four, finding his carriage almost empty, and opening the blinds as the train halted. The sun was shining at Marseilles station with a soft radiance he recalled from childhood, the air breathed a heady smell of flowers, and from the revived restaurant car came a nourishing smell of coffee. He could not at all afford breakfast on the train, but this return to France and to Mentone was, after all, a celebration. The cares of England and the war dissolved over his *café au lait*; the world seemed infinitely promising.

He had the key of the house from before the war, but did not think it would work. On arrival at Mentone, he was to go to the office of a lawyer who had charge of the family's estate and who had already made proposals for the sale of the property, should that be desired. Well, no doubt the place would have to be sold, his brother saw no alternative, it was quite impracticable for Francis and himself to maintain a large house in the South of France. They had very little money and what would they do with such an establishment?

He located the lawyer, who turned out to be friendly and glad to see him. As a very young man, working for a property agency, he had first shown the house to Charles's parents. *'Je me souviens bien de vos parents,'* he said, *'vos pauvres parents. Hélas, vous trouverez la maison assez triste — vous verrez — delabrée. Ils ont coupé les oliviers. Allons-y! Mais d'abord il faut que je vous donne une lettre, qu'on vient de recevoir ici. Je ne l'ai pas lue.'* The letter was from Tours, from the owner of a furniture repository, and told him that all the items Monsieur and Madame Williamson had deposited with him in 1939 remained in his care, in good condition. He was happy to say that the Germans who had visited his establishment hoping to confiscate the possessions of enemy nationals had not found them. He looked forward to receiving instructions. Charles almost wept and showed the letter to the lawyer, who smiled and remarked that there were indeed some good people in France and that Monsieur Williamson did not realise how fortunate the British were never to have suffered enemy occupation.

Then the lawyer drove Charles through the wan and battered streets of Mentone and along the promenade, pointing out the theatrical flight of steps from the sea front to the church of St Michel, which the Italians had constructed during the war. '*Pas mal, il faut avouer,*' he remarked, '*mais on a dû démolir un tas de bâtiments. Enfin les Italiens batissent mieux qu'ils ne se battent.*' He also pointed out the stump of the memorial to Queen Victoria, remarking only, '*Plus de Victoria . . . une plaisanterie italienne.*' When they arrived at the house, he deposited Charles and his small battered suitcase at the gates and drove off, advising Charles not to try to sleep in the house for the moment. '*Vous ne trouverez plus de gens à la maison,*' he said, '*mais à leur place, des rats . . .*'

The gate piers were worn out. No paint had been applied to them for years and most of the plaster had fallen off. The old iron gates with their rococo decoration had been stolen long since. Nobody could have driven a car up the torn potholed drive, on to which a couple of trees had fallen. The raised oval bank in front of the house was littered with decaying vegetation and odd pieces of furniture, kitchen cupboards, things he did not recognise. The palm tree, which rose triumphantly above the front of the garden, had not received its biennial pruning for many years. Beyond the curving staircase and the protective wall of shrubs he could glimpse disorder. But it was a promising disorder, dashed with flurries of colour, which reminded him of the well-tended terraces and the smiling ponds of his mother's garden, at its miraculous peak in March and April.

It was not all chaos. Someone — who on earth? — had swept the steps that led to the front door and the verandah in front of the house, over which the wisteria, the extravagant wisteria which always amazed visitors, frothed and cascaded. His mother had told him that on her first visit ever to the house it was the wisteria that persuaded her this was the house she must buy. She had had no doubts and in a way she had been right...

Would he look first at the house or the garden? The house. He dreaded going inside. The house must be faced.

The inside of the house was much dirtier than the garden. Someone had been camping there recently, the lawyer had warned him, refugees. They had been forcibly removed and the house as far as possible made good against their attempted return. The hall had sparkled with cleanliness in his mother's day. He thought to himself that the worship of domestic cleanliness for its own sake was perhaps the silliest of human aspirations, so routine and ephemeral, so feeble and uninteresting an attempt to create an orderly microcosm in a chaotic universe. Now the room contained a couple of broken down chairs, which perhaps he did recognise, and piles of newspapers and rags, which looked as though they had served as a bed. The grate had been used for a fire quite recently and beside it lay a book from which pages had been torn, for kindling he supposed. As for the floor – he preferred not to look too closely at the floor, where the old marble was hardly visible. It was returning to nature, this house, he thought. A few years more and the ceilings would collapse and trees would sprout within the walls and shoot out into the window cavities. Should it indeed be swept away? Were they right to think of obliterating this house of his childhood?

He opened the door to the large drawing room – at least the doors survived. As he did so, there was a sound of scuffling. It must be the rats the lawyer had spoken about. The room was completely dark, and smelt of damp and excrement. He lit one of the matches the lawyer had given him, and shuddered. In the candle's brief light he saw that this room, once the stage for social gatherings, had been desecrated. The walls were splattered with graffiti, the floor covered in rubbish, the mirrors broken, the chandelier, which had shone so genially on gatherings of Mentone's English society, gone. God, how large the room was, and how horrible. He could not face opening the shutters and seeing it in daylight.

The dining room was no more sympathetic. Where his parents had lunched and dined for twenty-eight years, only the parquet floor and the mild rococo decoration of the ceiling recalled the staid elegance he remembered. No furniture, several window-panes cracked, one or two disman-tled jugs and bowls (he supposed everything of that sort had been looted), packing cases, more piles of rubbish, a sweet smell of decay he did not care to identify. Ironic, in the temple of Hygeia his mother had created, to find her gods and goddesses brutally toppled.

Upstairs, more disorder. But he was struck by the number of books remaining from his parents' time, stacked in piles in the corridors, on shelves, thrust into cupboards. He discovered later that almost all the books had survived the war untouched by the Italian officers (who perhaps were no great readers of Henry James), but that many had later suffered on account of the luscious glue in their binding on which starved rats glutted themselves.

He left the house hurriedly, appalled. At the same time a corner of his mind was considering how the building might be converted to present-day conditions. The stairs at least were not touched. What had they thought of the place, he wondered, those soldiers rudely inhabiting rooms that had for so long served as shrines of domesticity? Had they been conscious of the house's charm or the garden's beauty?

The garden was not so bad. Many of the olive trees had been cut down, the ponds were full of weeds rather than water, the gravel paths were almost lost, but the irises struggled bravely through the grass, the shade of the pergola still contrasted with the brightness of the lawn, the cypress hedges raggedly suggested the order of earlier years. The garden was almost soundless: there was so little traffic on the roads now, and the house emitted none of the soft but insistent domestic sounds that had filled mornings and evenings in the old days. On either side he could glimpse the tumultuous gardens of the long-neglected neighbouring villas, and the sea and the mountain embraced the house as always. Yet among the disorder he could detect signs of re-emergent work, of flower-beds weeded, of walls where the tumbled stones had been propped into a semblance of neatness. The arum lilies his mother had planted, one of her last acts in the garden, were flourishing in the beds behind the house as though someone had tended them. Such flowers could scarcely grow without attention, surely?

Walking through the wild garden below the top wall of the property, he heard within the burgeoning silence a sound as of a person moving. Could this be so? He stopped. The sound stopped. He waited, sure that he was not alone in the garden. A refugee? One of the wretched people who sought flight from Italy in France, climbing dangerously over the mountains into the land of spurious promise? What should he do if he met such a person? Imperiously order him out of a garden that seemed scarcely to be Charles's property? Embrace him, share the sufferings of humanity? Hold an embarrassed conversation in the English manner?

Past one of the thickest bushes and round one of the few surviving olive trees, came a man. Short, dark, compact in build. Unfamiliar. The man stared at him, as though astonished and yet recognising the inevitable. Then, in the Mentonnais accent which sounded like Italian, he said, 'Monsieur Charles,' but doubtingly. Who now could use this form of address, one he had always hated but had not known how to avoid? 'Monsieur Charles,' said the man again, 'vous êtes bienvenu,' and held out his hands. Charles recognised him at last. It was his parents' under-gardener, Franco.

Franco wept. Charles, schooled not to weep, stared at him in amazed silence, advancing a hand and approaching hesitantly. He feared such physical contact with a man who had become almost a stranger but knew that offering a touch, even an embrace, was his duty. As he moved through the rich vegetation towards the performance of this highly charged greeting, he realised that this reunion was intended. The house and garden could not be abandoned. It was his obligation, he knew — though how many convictions of this sort turned out to be false — it was his obligation to return.

⊰ MARCH 1931 ⊱

HELEN WAS FAMOUS for what her husband called 'tiresome treats'. When guests wanted to read in the garden, or walk gently along the coast to the Rochers Rouges for a swim, or explore the Old Town, they would find that an elaborate excursion had been arranged. They were to be driven to Monte Carlo to see the princely aquarium, or made to take the omnibus to the lofty village of Castellar so that they could walk back down the mountain, or given a tour of the Roman sites of the vicinity. They could refuse, theoretically (the idea was always mooted in terms of 'I thought you might enjoy . . . but of course if you don't want to . . .'). But very few had the boldness to say no.

On this occasion Helen had excelled herself, Henry reflected. She had decided it would be a good idea if the boys met some of their cousins, and in particular some nice girls. It was, after all, the moment in their lives when they would be looking for girl friends (detestable phrase!), and neither seemed to have made much progress in that direction. She therefore reacted with pleasure – not echoed by her family, apart from Francis who dutifully tried (not very convincingly, Henry thought) to sound delighted – when she received a letter from Lydia Morris, a cousin of Henry's in Leicestershire. The letter asked if her two daughters could come and spend a few days with the Williamsons in

Mentone during the Easter holidays. 'So long since we all met...' said the letter, 'do think it would be fun for the young people... such nice girls, full of high spirits, hardly been abroad, and your boys much the same age...'

They had indeed come, for two solid weeks of the Easter holidays they had come. Charles, just down from Oxford and pursuing a literary career before he settled down to a proper occupation, and Francis, still at Cambridge, were told that they must without fail be at home while their cousins were in residence. They were not altogether ready for their cousins. Two English roses. Two English thumpers. They were the same age as their Williamson cousins. They loved the lawn tennis club. They were very good at bridge. They were not so keen on the richer sorts of foreign food (which they found 'a bit queer') or the Old Town, which they thought awfully sweet but smelly. When the customary springtime treat of going out after dinner to hear the frogs croak in the long pond was suggested, they giggled and darted looks at one another that suggested, 'Oh, aren't they funny?' They were much amused by Charles, whose doubts over whether he should pursue a literary or an artistic career did not seem to them of great importance. He was embarking on what was to become an extended passion for Cézanne, and tried to explain to them why he found the artist inspiring. They thought his attempts to expound the importance of the 'plastic sense' ludicrously amusing, and made jokes on the lines of ' "sezs she", "sezs who?" "sezs Anne" '. He soon desisted from his efforts. They did not. Francis, who talked from time to time about his enthusiasm for mineralogy, they found easier, especially since he was an excellent dancer and in the staidness of the drawing room danced with them for hours to the strains of Louis Armstrong on the gramophone. He looked very young for his age and they giggled afterwards about his smooth black hair and his touching eagerness to please, but they always chose him as a partner before his brother. Charles, who was less fond of dancing, would look moody during these proceedings and as often as possible would disappear with some improbable excuse.

To Henry they were extremely polite. He was not only master of the house but, as they unconsciously made clear on several occasions, immeasurably older than themselves. They addressed him as 'Cousin Henry', a title he much disliked but for which he could not contrive an alternative. They would never have called him by his Christian name.

One of these splendid sorts was called Rosemary. The other was Anne. They had both attended some sterling school in the English countryside, where they had had a ripping time. Helen listened with astonished revulsion to their stories of japes there, in which Charles (fascinated by their resemblance to girls in the stories of Angela Brazil) encouraged them: Helen had hated her days at boarding-school, heading all her letters from school and inscribing all her books 'In captivity'. Rosemary and Anne had never before been abroad, except once to Ireland to hunt. ('And d'you consider Ireland really is abroad? It's so like home,' one of them said to Henry, who had never been there.) They loved outdoor activities, which they pursued vigorously at Mentone, especially tennis and long walks up and down the mountains. There were, of course, no horses for them to ride: they were polite about this but clearly looked forward to returning to the pleasures of home. As they put it in the visitors' book, as part of a duet which they had composed (no doubt laboriously at night in the spare room, with much stifled mirth):

> We are hefty, we are horsey, we are hearty
> We rejoice in feeding fowls, and riding mokes,
> But we suffer silently with cocktails at a party,
> And laugh at all our host's historic jokes.

Beside this effort was a photograph of the two of them, in tweed skirts and jerseys and unostentatious pearls, scowling at the camera in the manner of well-bred English girls.

Everyone liked them, in principle. Francis did not at all mind, in principle, when they made him an apple-pie bed two nights running, and after a while even seemed to be becoming faintly partial to Anne, the younger sister, who was a good dancer and mildly less hearty than her sister. Charles showed no such weakness. Taught since childhood to conceal emotion, he learnt to assume a fixed grin when ribald discussion of 'plastic sense' came up. Helen professed to adore the girls and find them terrific fun, although the excursions she contrived became ever longer, ensuring they would be away for entire days while she remained at home. And as for Henry – well, he did not mind, indeed he enjoyed, the crack about 'historic jokes'. He could see that the jokes he told were out of date, going back to his days at school or university, and hardly in the vein of jokes told nowadays in England. Puns were no longer current, and the comic verses which, despite his family's protests, he liked to recite were hardly innovative.

What he could take less easily was the remark one girl made to the other as they were swinging down the stairs on their way to the tennis club, thinking they were not overheard: 'Did you hear what the old boy said to me yesterday?' 'The old boy' – oh, God, the Old Boy! This must be him, only fifty and yet already an Old Boy. Remembering this, the day they left, he looked again in the mirror in his room. His hair was indeed turning grey but he did not think that his shoulders were stooped or his eyes dulled. What was worse was the thought that he seemed so old to these heedlessly cheerful young women, that they felt obliged to be unfailingly polite, that his age apparently put him on a higher level to themselves – if 'higher' was really the word. They were so deferential, fetching his food at breakfast (they had refused breakfast in bed) and listening to him assiduously, and yet they never treated him, as he would have liked them to do, as one of themselves in the way that his sons, he realised, were generally kind and fond enough to do.

Glad to know that the girls had enjoyed themselves, Henry was even more glad they had gone. When he went into lunch the day they left and saw his assembled family, he knew he was not alone. 'I suppose we are very different from the society our cousins are used to,' he remarked to the company in general, 'and must seem very odd and even exotic – certainly eccentric.'

'Shall we not have any cousins to stay for a while?' said Charles to his mother. 'Our sensibilities are too delicate to stand the excitement. Unless they are over sixty and preferably lame.'

'Don't be so horrid,' she replied. 'Anne and Rosemary are extremely nice girls. Just because they aren't interested in art . . .'

But they all ate their *risotto à la Milanaise* with particular relish that day, Henry thought, and talked with more gaiety and lack of constraint than he remembered their doing for a long time.

⊷ RECOLLECTIONS ⊶

CHARLES WAS BORED by his family, he would say when asked about life at the house before the war. Old friendships, old ties were best forgotten when they lost their savour, when people once important to one faded into mere acquaintances, names in an address book, unless of course when resurrected as characters in a novel. Cousins who were only interesting (often scarcely that) by accident of birth, or flames of long ago with whom one had played tennis in summers long past or driven to La Turbie to see the sunset or to Monte Carlo for a flutter – leave them to the past, he would say, when his faithful, kind-hearted brother chided him for neglecting past friends. Life did not allow time for obeisance at the altar of faded friendships. It was too short, too precious, dedicated (in his case) to the understanding and creation of beauty, to be frittered away in meaningless social ceremonies. He had seen too much of those in his parents' existence, devoted particularly in later years to sociable rituals, rituals that bored and depressed him, filling him with contempt for the exchange of banalities and elevating physical necessities into the purpose of existence. This is not what I shall do when I can live as I choose, he would think angrily as a boy, listening to the conversation at those endless lunch parties of his mother's. Though the people were neither ill-natured nor stupid their conversation was confined in a cage of good breeding and the requirement to be pleasant and uncontroversial. Even during the 1930s, as political good manners were abandoned all over Europe, his parents appeared little inclined to discuss or think of anything more serious than problems at the tennis club and the local irrigation system.

When he went back to the house after the Second World War he divided it into flats, keeping only one for himself and letting out the rest. He spent much of the year there, particularly in the winter, leading sometimes a solitary life and sometimes sharing the flat with one of the girlfriends with whom he pursued brief and often complicated relationships. It was the ideal place in which to work, with no social obligations, and the town was cheap enough to allow him to eat his dinner at one of the small, not very good restaurants almost every evening. He would set himself the task of writing 1500 words a day and followed a little routine: five hours in the morning, a walk or some desultory work in the slightly shabby garden in the afternoon, another two hours' work in the early evening before a glass of wine and the walk out to the town. Routine, he found, averted depression.

Every so often a brown-paper package of books for review would arrive from London, or an issue of the *Times Literary Supplement*. He looked forward to these moments, which made him feel still a part of the literary life of the capital. When his own novels appeared, he would be sent the reviews by his publisher, an event he sometimes found horribly bruising since his novels wavered for a long time in the category of 'promising' without ever achieving the full-blooded recognition he hoped for. As time passed, he was never sure whether to try to be more experimental or more popular, and his publisher hardly assisted him by telling him to be himself. He briefly contemplated a novel about his parents but found the prospect too painful.

So, one way or another, he did not want to be reminded of the past life of the house. When in 1948, sorting through the attic while the house was being prepared for conversion, he found a trunk filled with albums and family papers, he could not bring himself to look at it. He thrust it into a *cabane* in the garden, as though it might conveniently disappear if not opened. Only a year or so later did he confront the case. He was working at the time on a woebegone and highly realistic study of bedsitter life in Bayswater (which was to turn out not a success) and the book was proceeding badly, so badly that he began to wonder if there was any point in finishing it. He thought as he opened the trunk that, though he might well throw it away, its contents should be checked.

To his surprise, the trunk did not contain many letters. He supposed his parents, both enthusiastic correspondents, had taken their letters with them to Pau, or had destroyed them. What it did contain, hardly damaged, were ten or twelve photograph albums, his parents' visitors' book, the sale particulars of the house from 1912, two stiff-backed exercise books. The latter seemed faintly familiar from the outside. He looked at them with the curiosity that the sight of an archive always aroused in him, mixed this time with apprehension.

The photograph albums he remembered well. His mother was attached to them in a sporadic way and would show them to guests, particularly the guests who came to stay for three weeks or so and after a while needed to be seriously entertained. The earliest album had 'Henry Williamson Christmas 1903' stamped in gold on its handsome leather front and illustrated his father's time at Oxford and particularly the merry stays he had enjoyed at Blithbury. Already at twenty-one he was a regular visitor there: several photographs showed him disporting himself with the youthful Helen. They would be punting on the lakes, or throwing themselves into poses that must have seemed comic at the time, or hurling snowballs at other well-dressed and happily laughing young people. It looked cheerful and confident, this way of life, but absurdly remote, and the initials below the photographs identifying the participants seldom meant anything to him. A photograph labelled 'Easter 1900 Blithbury' showed Henry, in a suit and tie as always but with his hair tousled and romantic disorder in his clothes, sitting on a bank and reading aloud to an admiring (and pretty) Helen. To their son, gazing at their image with characteristically equivocal emotion, they looked touchingly young and innocent.

One photograph showed Helen standing in a long white dress, being painted by an artist. He was amused to see it, since the portrait itself had lately been found in the attic, with several holes and looking much less splendid than when it adorned the drawing room before the war. He and Francis had agreed that there was little purpose in retaining so large and damaged an object (a shocking picture, too, in Charles's view, the worst sort of Edwardian society image). It had to be destroyed, though they toyed with the idea of cutting out the head and saving that. But in the end destruction had been settled on. Charles had sliced up the canvas and burnt it in the garden.

One album was devoted to India. It recorded jolly scenes in gardens, on verandahs, outside what seemed to be clubhouses. Ambala, Kasauli, Rawalpindi Club Park, the photographs were labelled, mysterious names that conveyed nothing to him. His parents had hardly ever spoken about India, as though their life there had been erased from their memories. Dutiful views of famous sights and mountains, with Simla looking like an Alpine resort under the snow. Many of these scenes were populated by his parents and by their friends who again would be doing amusing things, holding up huge fishes or appearing costumed as mysterious Oriental persons. Humour seemed to be the cement for these activities, larking about, keeping a sense of proportion, not taking anything too seriously, revelling in good-natured British fun (which foreigners, nice and clever as they often were, hardly ever got right – though, of course, they had their own style of humour). Humour had been a crucial prop in his father's later life, he considered. Jokes kept emotion at bay.

Of life in Mentone there were many more photographs. Numerous views of Francis and himself as boys, adorable in sailor suits, standing beside the car holding butterfly nets or dressed up for the carnival or posing with their father in the Piazza San Marco. Photographs of Winchelsea and Rye, of Chartres and Rouen, of Venice and Florence mingled with commercial postcards of famous sights, which conveyed instant *ennui*. The family had travelled every summer in the 1920s, taking long, cultivated holidays, staying at comfortable but not flashy hotels, sightseeing every morning and often in the evening too. Even his mother would emerge from her room at the early hour of ten to enjoy some especially fine church. There were several albums devoted to the First World War, as though this had been a period of particular significance for his parents. British officers consuming tea or holding the boys on their knees, French and Serb officers in orderly lines, Helen dressed as a nurse with ranks of other Florence Nightingales, and the inscription 'Dames de la Croix Rouge' beneath the photograph. Most of the groups were serious in presentation, but sometimes characteristic jollity broke in, with a central figure holding aloft some incongruous object such as a watering can. The hospital itself (a sumptuous hotel, evidently, before the war) played a major part in the albums. In its marble halls one could admire ladies doing war work, impeccably but not ostentatiously dressed, smiling at the world in a sisterly way or sewing in rooms filled with piles of linen. They were mostly older women, although in one photograph a young woman appeared, wearing a look of desolation that still spoke to the viewer. Ladies were also shown at home, in the garden or behind a crisply covered tea-table on the balcony. It was clear that wartime exigencies had not compromised the standard of hospitality at Lou Paradou.

Photographs of Japan and Australia were labelled 1919. The parents must have made a world tour but Charles could remember nothing about this enterprise. Obviously, he had not been included. Photographs of sociable activities continued through the 1920s and 1930s, picnics with friends such as the Knoxes. And there were the pictures of Pau, a surprising number of those.

Under these albums Charles, by this time nostalgic, reflective, still detached from the childhood and youth that seemed so distant, found two other books. One was the recipe book kept by the formidable and talented Madame

Amélie from Belgium, who had worked for his parents for almost twenty years. It must have been a happy household for the servants, he supposed, since they stayed for so many years. Dishes from all over the world were recorded in carefully inscribed French: pastas, Irish stew, moussaka from Egypt, *arroz con pollo*, dishes from Sweden, Greece, Mexico, English savouries and puddings (*pouding* Marmalade, *pouding* Cabinet). He recalled the food from his childhood without interest: he had despised it, so rich, so damaging to his mother's aspirations to beauty, so much discussed, so excessive.

Then there was the visitors' book. This began in 1905 and ended in 1940. It opened with a humorous drawing of a thousand ships *en route* to India transporting, it was rumoured, the luggage of an English princess travelling incognito from Staffordshire to Bombay. Visitors to the family in India recorded in drawings and verses jolly or calamitous events, disasters on excursions, a view of a garden from a verandah. In 1908 this period ended, with the move to England. More drawings, more jokey verses, a sketch by an artist showing himself drawing by the roadside long after he should have been back for dinner ... old forgotten gentle pleasantries, an undemanding life. Did he remember the names of these people? He supposed he did, but hardly could be bothered to try. And then the Mentone pages, where a steady but not strong current of visitors was recorded, six or eight each year. They often stayed for a month or so, regularly inscribing self-deprecating jokes about the length of their stay and the tedium inflicted on their hosts. In the 1930s his own friends began to appear, and Francis's. Many of those later visits he remembered vividly from the photographs, though he had not thought of them since. He closed the book.

Yet, though he might close the book upon them, when he was not busy or was consuming his solitary and exiguous dinners, he could not help recalling his parents' lives, more vividly than he had since their death. He had, he supposed, refused to let himself think about them, other than in the most practical terms. Thinking about them, he remembered with a sense of prickling shame the contempt he had felt for them, particularly his mother. He and his mother had never discussed the feelings between them: in the English manner both thought it better not to discuss personal problems openly. Instead, one hoped such emotions would soon be forgotten.

As for his father – well, he had always been fond of his father. The indifference and suspicion he had felt in his late teens and early twenties for this kind, reserved man had melted as he grew older. What had kept his father functioning, Charles wondered, through those long days of comfortable routine and order, those days dominated by discussion of domestic and social arrangements, constant demonstrations of affection and solicitude for Henry from his wife and, less effusively, for her from him, those days of tennis and dramatic entertainments and luncheons? What had his father thought about when he woke in the morning and contemplated another day of ease? 'What shall we do this afternoon?' – how often had that plaintive enquiry been made?

Sitting alone in the *petit salon* where his family had spent so many evenings beside the fire, Charles regretted opening the trunk. He had been right to think the past was better left as the past. This was a different age: people were no longer pushed by their wealth into leading lives of idle pointless comfort. The old wealth no longer existed, after all, and if it did the mood was different, people expected to work, men at least...

There was a third book. It was something they had thought lost, a book which in his youth was much discussed but seldom seen, though his father would sometimes read aloud from it. This was his father's 'Curiosity Book', a compilation of ghost stories and anecdotes he had made between 1917 (as an inscription announced) and his last years. It recounted strange happenings, divided into experiences told to his father at first hand ('story verified by questioning'), second hand or third hand. The source would be always scrupulously identified unless a note appeared, such as 'This story has no right here because I am not sure of its authority.' The events were not particularly frightening: mostly, unpleasant noises or apparitions, nightmares, strange coincidences. Some of the early stories from the First World War recorded the death and reappearance in spirit form of young people, whether killed in combat or by illness. There was a tale of two young men being asked to a ball in a strange city by an unknown woman. When they attended the ball, which was held in a large elegant house, one man left behind his cigarette case. He returned to the house the following day and found the building long derelict and wholly unequipped for a party – but there among the ruins was his cigarette case ... The meticulous index ordered the episodes by type of apparition. The book never revealed what the compiler thought of these events or whether he believed in them. What was the meaning, for example, of his cryptic note 'The great majority of the first-hand stories are quite pointless'?

Had his father ever intended to publish this compilation, as in the 1930s a similar compilation of anecdotally based ghost stories by Lord Halifax had been published? Charles thought not: such an action would have been too earnest and revealing. It was, after all, a curiosity book, an amusement — what would be gained by publication? Wasn't he working in the tradition of *belles lettres* writers who compiled commonplace books to fill the hours and keep the intelligence mildly exercised? If he had not been so damnably comfortably off, would his father have shaken himself out of indolence and applied himself to writing, like his son?

These reflections made Charles gloomy and he put away the volumes in a cupboard where he would not be reminded of them. There was no need for him to dwell on those wasted lives — his, after all, if not happy, was at least not wasted.

Bertha Morgan was engaged by my wife Helen Williamson as maid in 1912. She told me in about 1915 that when she travelled down to Blithbury Hall with my wife in 1912 she was met by the children aged three and two at the door. The same afternoon in the servants' hall she asked how many children there were and was told two boys. (Charles and Francis.) She said, 'But there was a girl too, older than the boys.' Our daughter Phoebe who died at six months old would have been five at the time.

We recollect that no girl child could have been there at the time come to play with the boys. The maid to whom Morgan spoke about the little girl said in 1915 that she remembered Morgan's question. Helen may have been thinking of Phoebe and influenced Morgan to 'see' her. But Helen does not remember thinking of Phoebe at that moment.

From Henry Williamson's 'Curiosity Book'

✦⟞⟞ 1936 ⟝⟝✦

From an unpublished essay on Blithbury Hall by Charles Williamson

...WE WENT THERE every year for our summer holidays. I do not suppose, now, that it was a very large house, but it seemed enormous then. I had a nursery on the top floor and every morning I woke up there, except for the day or two before the horrid end of the holidays, seemed a renewal of happiness. In my memory the sun always shone at Blithbury though I do not think there was really anything especially remarkable about the climate in Staffordshire in the 1920s.

My parents lived in the South of France for most of the year. It was their home, but for me home was not on the Riviera but at Blithbury. When I went there twice a year on leave from school, I would be looked after by my redoubtable aunt, who lived there all the time and was the merriest of spinsters. When the car collecting me from the station turned the corner into the little park and I saw the house in the distance I would feel I was back where I belonged.

I remember the house with almost painful clarity. I am sure it was Blithbury that gave me the feeling for beauty which for me is one of the most important values in the world. Everything there was calculated to please, from the panelled hall with its portraits of our rather brief lineage supplemented by a few eighteenth-century ladies and gentlemen who came with the house, to the narrow, creaking housemaids' corridor, scrubbed by generations of Staffordshire lasses. My aunt kept the house in impeccable order, and it was filled with a sense of cleanliness and care. It had a smell of beeswax, and soap, and roses, and old leather, at least I suppose those were the ingredients. I have hardly found that smell anywhere else and nowadays it probably scarcely exists.

The library was my favourite room. It had been added to an older house in the late eighteenth century, by James Wyatt we liked to think. It retained its original bookcases and a marble chimneypiece with rams' heads in the corners, and everything in the room, the curtains, the carpets, the backs of the books, seemed to have faded to the same soft honey colour. It had a large table for a dozen readers, but there were seldom any readers there apart from me. Even on the brightest days, when sun and sports beckoned, I found myself drawn to the library, wanting to read everything in the world, impelled by the pleasures and dangers and excitements awaiting me between the covers of books. It became known as my room, and when I was needed someone always looked for me in the library.

The garden I loved almost as much. The house stood on a little hill, with hanging woods (on a modest scale) beneath it. Stretching to the south was a series of lakes, connected by streams with little bridges over them. Huge elms overhung the lakes, and in summer when one rowed or punted around, one seemed to be in an enchanted landscape, shaded by great trees, with lapping water all around one and in the distance the prospect of smiling countryside where nonetheless giants might lurk. During those afternoons, the lakes would be almost silent, with only the wood pigeons to disturb the stillness.

Recently, the house was destroyed. Nobody wants to live now in a place devoted to beauty, and elegance, and peace. They prefer to live in bungalows along the arterial road. And with the house my childhood disappeared, too.

⤖ APRIL 1934 ⬸

From the diary of Anne Smith

3rd April 1934

Off to France tomorrow with Charles to stay with his
parents in Mentone. I'm very excited about it. It's
wonderful of Charles to take me there. I don't think he
has ever taken a girl home before, at least he says he hasn't.
Mummy was a bit surprised since I haven't known Charles
for long and he's only been to stay at home once. But she's
made enquiries which reveal that the Williamsons are
extremely nice people (did she really think they ran a
disorderly house or dropped their aitches?). So I will be all
right! I have bought several new frocks and a sun hat and
hope they will be suitable. Charles is so creative and
unconventional that I can't imagine what his family will be
like. He hardly talks about them, only saying how furious
he was that they had got rid of the family house in
Staffordshire which he had always loved.

4th April (actually written on the 12th)

Up early, and I take the train up from Warminster to be at
Victoria in time for the boat train. Charles is waiting,
looking very much himself, no attempt to look tidy.

Indeed he looked rather romantic, in a long black cloak and a black hat. I don't mind the lack of tidiness at all, rather the opposite. I told him he looked like a revolutionary and he was rather pleased and said, oh, well that's appropriate then. He has all his sketching materials and books et cetera in a large bag, otherwise almost nothing in the way of luggage. He also, rather surprisingly, has the tickets which he has managed not to lose. Blissful journey to Dover – Charles has such interesting things to say about the history of the places we pass, and talks about the tonal value of the fields in springtime and so on. It's quite fascinating. We talked about his painting – he says it is just a diversion, writing is what he is serious about and he wants to be known as a writer So he will be, I'm sure, being so talented. I must talk to him about not overwriting which he's still inclined to do. Anyway, he enjoys painting and apparently Mentone is the perfect place to do it.

The sea journey not so good since I am sick but Charles is not sick at all and cheers me up with jokes (some in rather poor taste) and observations about the effect of light on the sea. I clutch him when I'm feeling particularly sick. Actually I'm so tired now I can't write any more.

6th April (really)

Here I am in my perfectly delightful room at Lou Paradou, sitting in a huge bed covered in white muslin with large pink ribbons all over it. It's quite early in the morning so breakfast won't be brought to my room (I adore the luxury of it) for an hour or so. We arrived after a not very peaceful night in the wagon lit on something romantically called the Train Bleu. I was with a large French lady who snored almost all night but it was lovely arriving. Charles seemed pleased that I was pleased but not particularly cheerful to be going home, which I found surprising, given how beautiful the place is. When we arrived at Mentone Mr Williamson met us and was very kind. We drove to Lou Paradou and there was Charles's mother waiting on the balcony (I'm sure she must have been waiting) to wave at us. We had to go inside and wash our hands and gargle before we were admitted to the presence. This seemed unusual but apparently it's the rule and even Charles did it. She must be about fifty or a bit more, and has a sweet welcoming face. She and Charles greeted one another in an odd sort of wary way, rather formal, and then he introduced me, also rather formally. I had the feeling that this was an unfamiliar situation for him and he felt quite uncomfortable. But she could hardly have been more welcoming. When I said nervously, 'I am so happy to be here, Mrs Williamson,' she replied, 'Oh, you must call me Helen, we are not at all formal here, and I feel I already know you through Charles. We're so glad you're visiting us. Down here we're quite isolated from life in England. We love new faces.' Breakfast was laid on the balcony and though I had already breakfasted on the train it seemed rude not to have something and anyway it looked extremely tempting. Charles refused and said grumpily that no one could eat as much food as people do here and remain healthy. I had no problem in eating quite a lot, especially since he'd been extremely stingy about dinner the night before. What a bore it is that men are supposed to pay for things like dinner and girls aren't allowed to do as we want.

Charles and his parents don't seem to get on well together. He's very uneasy with his mother. He cuts her short when she's talking and laughs at her. I suppose we all do this kind of thing but somehow it has an edge when he does it. I do see she's rather irritating and perpetually worrying, never sits still (not mentally, anyway), and is always anxious about the next plan. She's kind to me though, and appears delighted that Charles has a girl with him, and isn't shocked that we're going off to Italy without a chaperone. Mummy doesn't actually know this because I told her that the Williamsons were coming to Italy with us. This is a bit of a lie because they're only coming as far as Genoa, which is about a hundred miles into Italy, and putting us on to the train to Venice, but I suppose my statement is accurate, strictly speaking. Charles says that young people of different sexes travelling together is perfectly normal in the natural scheme of things (whatever that may be) and that the idea of the chaperone is an outmoded bourgeois convention to be thrown on the scrap heap of history like so much else. (He loves talking like this, especially when I get him to make lists of things to be discarded after the great Communist Revolution — the capitalist system, of course, and the monarchy, table napkins, public schools, sweated labour, hereditary titles, Jane Austen, the professional army, servants . . .) Since it's so terribly nice being with Charles

I'm inclined to agree with him. He's wonderfully liberating, I must say.

Mrs W knows all about Venice and has lent me several books about the city in the eighteenth century and Goldoni and Casanova. So I am reading hard, which is easy because nothing much happens here in the morning and Charles likes to write or paint and Mrs W doesn't appear. The person I see most is Mr W who likes to talk about books and has offered to show me his own library which we'll do tomorrow. He is very friendly but reserved, and doesn't like to talk about himself or what he did when he was young. Oh, and he is going to play the piano to me. From what I have heard, he's keen but not very accomplished – lots of expression and wrong notes.

Life here is very organised. Plenty of meals. You have to be dead on time, like at home, and you have to eat quite a lot too, or Mrs W is disappointed and says the cook will be upset. Charles is sometimes surly at these meals, and complains about how much time they take, especially at lunch. Lunch is quite long and complicated (and delicious) and he hates spending so much time on it because he likes to paint or write for as many hours as he can. But if you are late there can be trouble. Today we were late for tea after going for a long walk in the Old Town in Mentone. When we came back Charles was very nonchalant and hardly apologised. Mrs W was furious and said Charles showed her no respect. He was cross too and told her that she had no sense of proper values. I said it was all my fault and I'd insisted on a diversion that had made us late. Charles became even crosser and declared dramatically that typically I was entering into a dialogue about the apportionment of guilt, which was irrelevant since the only issue at stake was a minor matter of social convenience. Then he ate a cucumber sandwich in a vicious way as though he hated it and declared that living in a house with servants made life horribly constricted and you could never do what you wanted but always had to interrupt your activities for lunch or tea or dinner and such a life was like walking a treadmill and the only point of this routine was to provide a structure for people who didn't have enough to do. She got rather red in the face and said he was very rude and ungrateful and would not like having no servants and preparing his own food. So Charles stopped eating the sandwiches, pushing away the plate (which was practically empty because he'd eaten so many) with an air of disgust, and announced that he had no servants in London and was perfectly happy and disapproved of exploiting people merely because the current labour market made it easy. They went on like this for some time. Then they saw me looking miserable and stopped.

I hate this arguing. It was sad because we'd had such a wonderful walk in the Old Town. Charles talked about the history of Mentone and told me about the little republic and how it briefly gained independence before throwing in its lot with France in 1860, which some people still thought was a mistake. The town has a very special feeling, he said, if you know how to look for it. He said people like his parents hardly ever go into the Old Town, which they regard as dirty and full of bandits and dangerous smells. At one level Mentone is full of English people and other foreigners, and there are the French bourgeoisie who live here or visit and aren't particularly interesting (or so he says — how does he knows this?). But under these layers an old-fashioned life is still led by the local inhabitants who've always lived here. They're not well off but they survive. They speak a special *patois*. It's easy to recognise them, he says, just by looking at them in the street.

7th April

We went to Monte Carlo today and had a little flutter. I won a bit, Charles lost a bit. Helen told me before we went about a friend of theirs, an Englishwoman (from a very good family, she said) who had married a wonderfully romantic Russian prince. He had no money but she had quite a bit and he gambled it all away, always using his special scientific gambling methods, which changed a good deal and sometimes helped him win but not often enough. After about three years there was no money left. So she had to keep them alive by teaching English to French people and sewing (which was one of the few things she'd learnt in the stupid school she had been sent to by her very good family) and even cleaning people's houses. After a bit he got bored with not being able to gamble or spend anything since she had become very fierce about the money she did have. So he left her, just disappeared one night and took her jewellery with him. They had no children and she didn't want to seek charity from her family. So she killed herself, since she saw no point in living any more.

I don't know why Helen told me this story, perhaps as a warning against gambling, but it had a depressing effect. In any case I'm much too boringly serious-minded to want to gamble in a big way and this evening Charles showed no interest in it at all, especially since he lost three times in a row as soon as he started. We looked at the other people, who were a sorry bunch, enough to put anyone off. Monte Carlo is meant to be very glamorous but to me it represented the ultimate in futility.

We were back in time for dinner, having had permission to miss tea. Both Charles and his mother made jokes at lunch about the importance of regular meals and the horrors of missing them, referring I suppose to yesterday. Jokes are what keep people together in an organised family like this, smoothing over the tensions.

The pasta here is delicious. I wish we ate more of it in England. And I do like drinking wine all the time, though I think that Henry isn't very interested in it. It's not very special here, certainly not as good as Father's.

It's clear that Henry and Helen, though they lead rather conventional narrow lives (as Charles reminds me from time to time), are intelligent and original and open-minded people. I just wonder, if they'd chosen to live somewhere stimulating and mixed with interesting people and perhaps even worked, whether they would have been happier. I don't think they're happy now, really.

They certainly enjoy conversation. I think they like me because I'm not stupid, and feel easy with me because I'm a little older than Charles. We had an interesting conversation about him the other day, when he wasn't there. Helen explained that they'd wanted him to go into the Diplomatic Service which they thought would be suitable, similar to his father's and grandfather's career but not forcing one to spend one's life in India. He begged to be allowed to write when he left Oxford and they said he could have a year to do so, with an allowance from them, as long as he took the Diplomatic Service exams at the end of that year. So he settled down to write and published a few articles and reviews and they were terribly pleased. Helen proudly showed me her book of cuttings from his publications, with everything dated and one or two enthusiastic comments made by her in the margins. At the end of the year I don't think anyone mentioned the Diplomatic Service again.

We talked a bit today about Francis, the younger brother. He has just started doing research at Cambridge in some sort of chemistry laboratory. Charles was vague about what he was doing, I suppose he doesn't think it's very interesting. Helen is obviously devoted to Francis, who seems to be a good-natured sort of person and very attentive to his mother – she's had at least one letter from him since we've been here. I think the brothers are rather competitive, even though they don't know it. Certainly I've never been introduced to Francis, though I've known Charles now for at least six months. I must do something about it, I'm sure it would be good for Charles to have an easier relationship with his family.

Am I in love with him? Yes, I think I am. I'm really not sure, it's quite odd. Is he in love with me? Not sure about that, either. He's certainly extremely fond, and attentive, and feels happy being silent with me, which is a good sign,

I feel, in someone who's so concerned with words. But love? Meeting his family helps me to understand him but I don't know that it makes him seem easier.

Would I like him to be less complicated? No, I don't think so. I like him as he is. Do I want to change him at all? Well, maybe. Do I feel sorry for him, in that annoying way I have? I think not, he's not really a person who wants people to feel sorry for him.

I suppose I just don't know how interested he is in people. His writing is the thing, isn't it? And his politics? Ah, well, we'll see . . .

April 8th

A very bad day. If there is one thing I hate it's a family row. My own are bad enough with Father and Edgar but listening to other people's is worse especially if you're in love (love?) with one of the people taking part. At lunch I was very much enjoying the *moussaka égyptienne*, which I've never eaten before, when the conversation turned to our departure for Venice two days later. Helen was looking forward, she said, to driving us to Genoa and staying the night, but she wanted us to delay for a day or two, since the day we'd chosen was her *jour de repos*. This means she stays in bed all day and rests (I don't know what she rests from, since she leaves everything to Miss Gordon who has to pretend that Helen is actually organising everything). Fine, said Charles, couldn't she have her *jour de repos* on another day? '*Repos* can always wait, can't it,' he added disagreeably, 'unless you're addicted to it.' He seems to swing backwards and forwards in his attitude to her, from being sympathetic to being horrid. She said all the arrangements had been made and that it was important for her to rest on a regular basis. Charles sneered at this. I hadn't seen anyone sneer properly before but he did it pretty effectively and it didn't look pleasant. He said all our arrangements had been made too, and couldn't easily be changed at the last minute. 'You don't understand, Charles,' she said. 'I am not a well woman, and I have to take care.' 'You certainly do look after yourself,' he said, 'no worries about that.' Henry looked pained and said, 'Charles, don't . . .' but never explained what Charles was not to do. Helen, who had been eating furiously all through this conversation as though her sanity depended on it, finally put down her fork and said, 'You can't always expect everything to be done in a way that suits you, Charles. You must sometimes accommodate yourself to others.' On which Charles stood up, threw his napkin at the table and shouted, 'How can you of all people have the cheek to say that? You're the most selfish woman I've ever met.' Then he stormed out of the room, slamming the door. There was a ghastly silence. I felt angry with Charles but rather sympathetic too, because she does make life so complicated. 'Does this little discussion put us off our lunch?' Henry asked me, slightly ironically, I thought. 'No, no, we must continue our lunch,' said Helen. 'Poor Anne must be fed properly after all her excursions and Madame Amélie will be very upset if we send the food back and will think she's cooked disastrously. I'm so sorry about all this.' And after a minute she said that she'd have to go upstairs and see to her face and out she went, heaving a bit like a grampus. Horrid of me to be unkind.

Henry rang the bell for the maid, who came in looking agitated having heard all the shouting I suppose. 'Only two for dessert,' said Henry, and to me he said, 'We will have to eat for two, Anne. It would never do to disappoint Madame Amélie, and eating is an important ritual here, especially since we hardly go to church.' And then he changed the subject.

After lunch Henry asked me how I was going to amuse myself. We sat for a while on the verandah talking about books. He is very interested in classical history although often interrupting his talk to say how out of touch he is, and far removed from the scholarly or literary worlds. He and Helen read novels together a great deal, Henry James and Edith Wharton and Aldous Huxley (who, I believe, lives somewhere around here though they don't know him). And the nineteenth-century Russians, and Balzac. Henry is very perceptive, though shy of offering his views until he forgets to be self-conscious. I don't know how much opportunity he has here to talk about books and such things other than in a superficial way at these lunch parties they have. We chatted on until about half past three when he said, 'Oh, God! I should have gone up to see Helen. I quite forgot, I was so much enjoying myself – will you excuse me?' and off he went. To console her, I suppose.

In the garden I found Charles sketching. He looked very surly when I approached, as though he expected me to criticise him – not surprising, really. I didn't say anything other than to ask if I might sit beside him while he worked. Yes, he said, if I didn't chatter. So I sat perfectly still, knowing he would talk to me in a while. Quite soon he asked, 'How was lunch in its terminal stages?' I told him his mother had gone upstairs and that I'd talked to his father about literature and Ford Madox Ford, a particular favourite of his, whom they knew during the First World War when he visited the house as a wounded officer and used to write in the garden. 'Yes, Pa's good on the books, isn't he?' he said.

Then there was another silence, and he started to paint again. He looked less anguished than before. I intended to scold him but thought it could wait. After a while he said, 'I suppose you're going to scold me?' So I told him I was thinking how best to do it. He said, 'You don't need to scold me, I know I behaved badly. I know I often do treat Ma unkindly. I do love her in an instinctive sort of way and I see she needs looking after but I can't stand the way she lives. I just can't bear the demands she makes of everyone and the unnecessary coddling and the pointless comforts and the joylessness of the whole life here. And I hate to see my father surrendering his independence and leading this absurd life. And . . .' and he was about to go on but I told him to hush. He looked hurt so I said that he should tell me about his feelings when we were in Venice and away from here, where it was all too intense. To which he replied, 'Oh, in Venice there are much more interesting things to do than think about my stupid family. But you're probably right, my Chelsea Athene,' which is what he sometimes calls me, rather irritatingly I find, it sounds so academic and unspontaneous. And he went on, 'I hope the scene at lunch didn't upset you too much. It must have been horrid to see us scrapping and mewling, particularly me.' 'I don't like to see you unhappy,' I told him. At which he smiled and kissed my knee, which happened to be close to his face, we were sitting on a flight of steps, and he said, 'That's comforting. Then I won't be.' Then we sat for a while in a companionable way and in a bit he said, 'You know, when I was a boy she never really liked me. I don't understand why not, but she never really did. I was a threat, I don't know. The one she loved and still loves best is Francis, dear little Francis, so good, so loyal.' I told him not be so sarcastic and disagreeable, it didn't suit him.

I don't really understand Charles at all, I have to say. I always feel a distance between us, however affectionate he is. He always seems to be watching himself, and me, and the way we are together. I don't know what will become of us.

9th April

Muted friendliness today among the Williamsons. Helen has graciously shifted her *jour de repos* to two days later, and we're all going to Italy together after all. It's like the move from the Gregorian to the Julian calendar, all this shifting around of dates. I persuaded Charles to use a bit of guile, and to say to her in a winning way (which is no problem for him, if he chooses, I suppose I may not recognise when it's being done to me) something on the lines of 'Ma, I do hope you might consider arranging things so that you can come with us to Genoa. It would be such a pleasure and would remind me of all the happy times we had in Italy with you when we were children.' I think he meant it, too, in a way. He uttered this after breakfast today when Helen emerged in her morning outfit. She looked immensely pleased and touched and said she would think about it — and yes, the impossible became possible. So they are coming, and spending a night in Genoa, in the best hotel, which they know they can rely on.

Lunch much calmer today. We talked about Venice, and Thomas Mann. A good deal of reading goes on in this house — just as well, not much else does.

After lunch Helen remarked to me (as she'd already done, several times) that she'd like to take me for a walk along the boulevard to see the cemetery, if I didn't know it already. No, I'd not been there and thought it sounded rather a gloomy expedition. She made it clear from her tone that this was to be a ladies' outing. After lunch it's thought essential here to sit down for a while and perhaps snooze after eating and drinking so much. But after half an hour of post-prandial stabilisation we set off, suitably guarded with coats and scarves against the cruel winds of April. (Actually the weather is divine.)

It was not altogether cheerful. We walked along the boulevard de Garavan, a pretty road made it would seem for walkers as much as motor-cars or carriages. It twists along the coast and gives unexpected views of gardens and little orange groves and vegetable gardens and the backs of the hotels and villas. Helen imparted details of the people she knows or knows of who live in some of the houses, and showed me the house of the Duchess of Sutherland (who's sold the place now) and the Baron de Lesseps, who built the Suez Canal, and the local English hotelier. She urged me to exclaim about the beauty of the coast, which I did willingly and often. She started by walking slowly as though with difficulty, but after a while seemed to forget this was necessary and stepped out in quite a bold and vigorous way. After about half an hour we arrived at the outskirts of the town proper, which is heralded by the cemeteries. We made a brief and dutiful tour of the war tombs – they did not seem to hold any special interest for her, lucky woman, though she told me about some of the soldiers they'd looked after in the First World War who had died in Mentone, though she had trouble remembering their names. Then we moved on to the graves for foreigners, especially the Protestants and Orthodox. They are set magnificently on a hill above the town, with immense views of the sea. The foreign tombs are reached through a curious necropolis, which contains the tombs of what I suppose are the major Mentone families. In many cases these are large marble temples with the name of the family inscribed over the door and iron gates between pillars, and photographs of the deceased in little oval frames, generally looking well-fed and owl-like. The foreign tombs are mostly more modest, and for me more poignant. Russians, Swiss, Scandinavians, Germans, people of all ages, many young when they died, and quite a few children. Lots of English and Scots and Irish. It's so sad to think of them travelling down to this sunlit coast where they thought they would be saved, and finding that

salvation eluded them even beside this smiling sea –
except, as the inscriptions reiterate, for the greater
salvation they will attain in Heaven. The cemetery is very
well kept, and the cypresses give it a mournful but
decorous character, and the sculpture is provincial but
looks well against the sea, and of course the sea itself is
spectacular from the top of the hill. I enjoyed it in a
dreary way.

Helen and I moved slowly up and down, she apparently
wanting to stay close to me. I felt I ought to be wearing a
long black dress with a black veil and little lacy gloves but
stupidly hadn't brought the right outfit with me. She
talked a bit in a funereal sort of way. 'It is so peaceful, so
restful, the most beautiful place in the town. They must lie
here so happily,' she said. 'I knew a few people who are
buried here. It would be a fine place to spend the years
after death.'

There is a peculiar custom here by which you can buy
the right to keep your grave for eternity, or till the Last
Trump, I suppose, when you wouldn't need it any more.
So quite a lot of the tombs have '*Concession à Perpetuité*' and
a number inscribed on them. It all looks rather
business-like and lacking in sentiment – but I suppose it's
nice if you're rich to know that you won't be thrown out
of your grave after twenty years. The Williamsons want to
be buried in England, she told me, as plainly as possible.
Apparently they talk about it quite a lot.

J. R. Green, the Victorian historian, is buried in the
cemetery. We looked at his grave, handsome and inscribed
'Historian of the English People – He Died Learning'.
Helen remarked to me, 'I expect you know his work. He

was extremely brilliant, you know, but his health forced him to live here a good deal and he died in Mentone. He hated the invalid community, as he saw it. He wrote a strange thing about the mountains behind the town. He said that for people who could never hope to climb up them they were prison walls. Did you know that?' I had to say no, I didn't.

On the way back to the house Helen began to talk more freely. She asked me about myself and my parents, and said she hoped one day we'd all meet. They come to England every summer for three months or so. I don't know what Mother and Father would make of the Williamsons, who are certainly not interested in country pursuits in the way they are. She said, as she has before, how pleased she was that Charles and I had met. Then she stopped. A moment or two later she asked me, 'You must think our life is dreadfully slow. It must seem very parochial to someone like you, in publishing and at the heart of the London literary world. Henry so much enjoys talking to you, you know, it's so stimulating for him.' And before I could reply the poor woman went on, interrupting her walk and gazing over the sea, 'It is so hard, sometimes, living down here, to know what the point of one's life is. We are forced to live here, of course, on account of our health, but we make very little contribution to the life of the place. I suppose occasionally we provide a refuge for some of the English people here but that's not very important, is it? You don't mind my saying all this, do you?' she went on. 'You are so sympathetic and kind.'

We walked in silence and then she stopped again and

pushed her parasol into some sand on the pavement and said, 'It was very sweet of Charles to say that he would like us to come to Genoa with him — did you suggest it?' So I found some sort of white lie, and she went on, 'He doesn't really want us hanging about, I'm sure. He'd much rather be with you and enjoy everything without his parents at his elbow.'

We walked on slowly. She seemed abstracted, and not willing to engage in normal conversation. My occasional openings were hardly acknowledged. Then she announced, 'You know, my dear, I sometimes wonder what point there is in my being alive. No one really needs me, in the great world or even in my own family. Henry would say he depends on me but actually he'd probably be better off without my worrying at him all the time. And do the boys need me, now that they're grown up? I try to show how much I love them, because I think that's important for a mother to do that however old one's child may be. I don't know how much they welcome it — perhaps Francis does. They're grown up now and don't need an old mother fussing over them...' She was crying by this time and I put my arm round her but could not think what to say. 'I'm quite useless, really, though everyone's too kind to say so,' she went on, 'just a burden on all these people who have to look after me. And as I grow older I shall become more of a burden, an old bore, and forgetful. Don't get old, my dear...'

The awful fact was that everything she said seemed to be true, but that was hardly the thing to say. So I told her how kind she had been to me, and how much I appreciated this. To which she replied that I was a dear girl, and that being kind to me came naturally, like breathing. Then she stopped crying, and we walked back to the house, and she resumed her intensive analysis of the properties we passed.

I think I understand her better. I feel sorry for her. I feel sorry for them all.

Charles was very brisk this evening, asking me if I've read the Baedeker to Genoa and Liguria, and how can I enjoy Italy if I don't do my homework properly? He hasn't packed yet, as I pointed out to him, and he mustn't hold us up in the morning.

10th April

Which he did, but not much, since I found most of the things he had lost and was anxiously seeking with many oaths and cries. He looked so sweet as he rushed up and down the bedroom corridor, so very thin with his red hair standing on end and his shirt not properly buttoned in the hurry and his eyes very bright. The things he was looking for were lying in a pile in the passage under a discarded mackintosh. We all drove to Genoa, and had a blissful day. The principal historic street, the via Garibaldi, is quite magnificent, we visited the Palazzo Rosso and the Palazzo Bianco, which are both art galleries, cathedral ancient but a jumble, lots of interesting churches notably Santa Maria di Castello. Helen and Henry are passionate sightseers, full of information and enthusiasm, eagerly reading aloud to one another from guidebooks and very light-hearted. Dinner at the hotel, very cheerful. They paid for our rooms thank goodness, which meant that we were comfortable.

11th April

More sightseeing in the morning. Huge but hurried lunch, mountains of saffron rice, then they saw us on to the train. I got affectionate embraces from both the parents, and felt horrid for having been in the least critical of them. Now, Venice . . .

Letter from Francis Williamson to his parents

Cambridge,
8 May 1936

Dear Ma and Pa

I'm just packing up my digs here which seems odd after three years in the same place. Amazing how much rubbish one collects. I'm being very ruthless and throwing away all sorts of things, old clothes and party invitations and magazines and odd screws and nuts and bolts which somehow one thought might be useful but never are. But of course I'm not throwing away anything to do with you, particularly not your letters (have just signed a contract with Pickfords for three vans to remove Maternal Correspondence to new residence).

I think it's high time I left Cambridge which no longer seems very interesting, particularly since there are so few girls around and practically none in the chemistry laboratories at all. The men are very nice and I shall miss them but not that much.

I had a goodbye cocktail party the other day. It was a bit chaotic since I held it in my rooms which are not very big as you know. My friend of whom you do not approve was there but not playing the lead role you will be glad to hear. I gave them gin slings, which were a big success – in fact all those research scientists became completely drunk and fell about on to the precious occasional tables given to me by doting parents. No damage actually. In the end I had to push them out of the door. Well, I suppose there will be no more of this sort of thing when I am a respectable civil servant.

Charles said he was coming but rang up at the last moment to say he was too busy. But Anne did come, and apologised for him and said he really did have awful deadlines to meet. She is so nice and straightforward, though I don't know that he cherishes her as he should. Anne had never been here before and I think she was curious to see what my rooms were like. As I said to her, 'They are barbaric,' and by the end of the evening I'm sure she agreed. We went out afterwards to have something to eat without the unmentionable one (with whom I had had a bit of a row in the kitchen during the party and she stomped off whirling her cloak, I'm sick of her to tell you the truth). A very nice new friend of mine called Lucy who is a teacher came instead. I know you'd like her.

I am so sorry I couldn't come out at Easter this year but I'm sure you understand why. But I will be out in the autumn, and much look forward to seeing you in London or wherever you choose to alight during the summer. I do hope you're both happy and not too busy or unwell or whatever. I'm very excited about my new life in London – I'm starting the job in a month so I shall be able to do some really good sailing with Angus and Jamie before I settle in.

Much love as always

F

⊰ 1937 – AN AUTUMN NIGHT ⊱

AFTER MIDNIGHT there was hardly any noise in the garden. The rustling in the wilderness and under the great palms continued all night; so did the soft splashings in the ponds. Occasional sounds of water pouring or windows opening came faintly from the house. The sleeping town was almost silent, and at dead of night few cars drove along the road that led to the bridge and the route to Italy. Only at certain hours was the quiet broken by the aggressive noise of the express train that hurried to Ventimiglia then abruptly expired. As soon as it passed, the embracing bushes and the terraces settled back into stillness.

The house was asleep, though perhaps not at peace. In the servants' wing at the back, which enjoyed the view of the Old Town that Helen had admired on her first visit, the cook, the parlourmaid and the housemaid each occupied a plain room with a high ceiling and red-tiled floor. Madame Amélie hardly stirred, dreaming of menus more exotic even than those she already devised in her taste for experiment and her desire to please appreciative employers. In the next room lay Victorine. To her, sleep came only from time to time. Drowsily she worried about her family up in the village of Castellar, and the problems of her nephew and his fiancée, and her old mother who nowadays never came down to Menton and had to be visited every week. And she worried about Monsieur and Madame. They looked, she thought, less happy than they should, anxious, even haunted. At meals (she could understand some of their English, and when she was in the room they often slipped into French to include her in the conversation), they discussed the political news of the day, the possibility of war, the League of Nations, Italy. She knew they must be thinking about the nearness of the frontier and the great defensive line the French had built along the mountains. 'You are so fortunate, Victorine,' Madame had said, 'to have your family so close. Our relations are so far away.' But then war was most unlikely, they would always conclude: nobody wanted it, and Mr Chamberlain was so sensible. Well, Victorine would not retreat to Castellar, in the event of disaster: she would accompany her employers wherever they took refuge, even if it meant going to England. If they wanted her, of course. And in that thought she found comfort and fell back to sleep.

In her handsome room with the white marble chimney-piece and the parquet floor, Betty seldom suffered dreams, or at least no dreams she remembered. She had retired this night to bed at half past eleven, after an hour or so of quiet reading and correspondence, orderly ablutions and an address to the Presbyterian God. She found herself in her dreams imagining their little household established in another house, a quite unfamiliar one. There she was supervising the domestic arrangements in a semi-alien kitchen, half the room she knew and half another one, where doors opened in the wrong place and a figure in whom she thought she recognised Madame Amélie spoke to her in broad Scots. Her reason told her as she slept to ignore such imaginings but her dreaming body moved from the kitchen down an unfamiliar passage hung with paintings of Lou Paradou, into a room where Helen and Henry were sitting in armchairs in a strained, uncomfortable way, not turning as she came in, not acknowledging her, so that she did not know whether these figures were indeed her friends. When she spoke their names her voice echoed as though in a vast empty chamber. She woke, furious with herself for breaking her sleep in the middle of the night, something she never did. The air seemed cold, for the first time that autumn. She turned on the light and reached for the novel she never seemed to have time to read.

There was no novel-reading in the tower room, the absurdly high room with its great windows looking on to the Old Town and the sea, isolated at the top of the square tower, which gave the house its Italianate quality. It looked like a house in a painting by Claude Lorrain, as Henry would remark, 'though probably not one of his best'. In the single bed thought suitable for an unmarried son, surrounded by the impeccable neatness which marked a man whose favourite recreation was to sail and whose yacht must always be kept in order, Francis slept. He dreamt confusedly but not disturbingly, about a woman he loved, about his boat, about the Mediterranean. He felt tonight that he was at home in a way he hardly ever felt, even now that he was grown up, away from this house.

His father dreamt of home too. The home he returned to in his dreams was a house he had known in childhood, though not very well. He saw himself in the Suffolk vicarage which his parents, on leave from India, had rented when he was a small boy. They only spent a few months at that house but for him it epitomised happiness and security. The sun was always shining there, but softly; the garden was always filled with flowers. In his dream, his mother, his distantly remembered mother, would be sitting under the lime tree in a great straw hat, with his distinguished alarming father beside her, reading aloud from some book or other. Henry would emerge from the house and move towards them. Encouraged by her waving, and the way she held out her arms, calling to him, he would take courage and run towards her, gathering extraordinary speed as he flew across the grass. But as she grew nearer and he gained the shadow of the lime tree, the rich dark shadow that enveloped him, he realised something had changed. His father turned away, no longer smiling, and as Henry stared at his mother's face he realised that she too was no longer looking at him. Her face was sinking into the face of another woman, a woman he recognised too well from the last years of his father's life when she had kept the family away from the retirement house in Bournemouth. But the bitter fear of this memory would pass, and his half-waking reason would tell him that he was safe, and adult. He would sink into somnolence and return to that rosy garden where once he had watched a black and purple butterfly hovering above a buddleia, and had known that he was experiencing a moment of perfect happiness.

Helen had plunged into sleep the moment Henry left the room after reading to her. Her dreams were scattered, flecked with fragments of conversation, crowded with problems that she sorted out to the amazement and delight of all who beheld her. Airily she enters the drawing room of Lou Paradou, which is filled with fashionable people who she realises suddenly are her friends, such people as the Bishop of Gibraltar and Noël Coward and the Duchess of Sutherland and Somerset Maugham, drinking cocktails out of tiny glasses and laughing vivaciously as they whirl cigarettes on long holders in the air. As she comes into the room they turn towards her, gazing in delight at her beautiful rustling white gown, and fall silent for a moment, the silence which means that a whole roomful of people is fascinated by the person who has just entered. As one, they burst into applause, hurling their glasses into the air so that they shatter with sharp noises like bullets hitting the ceiling. Are they firing bullets from the Berceau? – which still after all these years she has not climbed though she tries to, wearing heavy boots and a big helmet over her white dress, with Henry in front of her and Victorine behind pushing her and saying, '*Madame est trop lourde*,' from time to time. She reaches only a little way but the mountain is so steep and unwelcoming and she can go no further and now she never will climb this unmanageable height since it is covered in gun emplacements, the Fascists have made it almost into a fortress with barbed wire, sealing off Italy, and she will never climb the Berceau which overhangs her precious house with the guns pointing down into her garden where her family and her faithful dear servants are quite at the mercy of the soldiers. Francis who has just arrived that evening and seems so well and it is such a pleasure to see him though one wonders about whether he will be all right in difficult times ahead, Francis will be all right since he will escape in a yacht, kind loving tender Francis, he will embark on his little yacht if the Italians invade and sail off into the sea and would she accompany him would she find happiness on the sea at last and she steps off the quay with only the smallest bag in her hand and into his yacht while he encourages her smiling from the bridge but when she is on board the yacht becomes large and black swelling as she looks at it and as she climbs on to the deck a door slams and Francis is no longer to be seen his kind face invisible and the boat advances into the ocean purposefully as though escaping the gunfire and there is no one on board not even Henry whom she last saw on the balcony at home writing a letter and she wonders if she is suitably dressed for yachting since she is wearing only her underclothes how has that happened but she does not mind in particular and the boat moves faster into the storm its deck becoming lower and lower and nearer to the sea and she knows now that she is going to drown but she does not mind since it is inevitable and she is going to drown in the sea which she has looked at in admiration for so many years and which when you are actually upon it is no longer smiling and blue but black and harsh and she drowns

happily she drowns sinking full fathom five into the bosom of the sea her sorrows pouring from her fingers and her toes into the warm caresses of the water

Nobody in the house is aware of the territory outside. In the darkness of the night the well-ordered garden recedes in time, past the splendour of its botanical finery, past the terraces cultivated by peasants, into a wild sweet paganism where the whole world passes along the Roman road to Italy but does not linger. Had those dreaming gentle people at Lou Paradou stepped outside their nocturnal shelter or even looked from their window, they might have sensed the menace that stirred outside, beyond the polite bounds of their domesticity.

⊰ DECEMBER 1937 ⊱

THE FIRST ARRIVALS back from the theatre are Mrs Williamson and Francis. As they come up the stairs he holds her elbow as though to steer and calm her, looking extremely anxious as he often does. She hurries into the house, breathless and also anxious.

'Victorine, Victorine,' she cries. 'C'est tout prêt? Tout va bien?'

'Tout va bien, Madame. Et la pièce — on a bien joué? On a bien applaudi?'

'C'était un succès fou,' Francis assures her. 'Full house — comment dit-on ça? Le théâtre était complet. Ils ont ri comme des fous.'

'Et les serviettes, Victorine, où sont les serviettes?'

'Les serviettes sont ici, Madame, comme vous avez demandé.'

'Pas besoin de m'inquiéter, Victorine, puisque vous êtes là. Mais avec Betty au théâtre . . . Francis, we've not had so many people to the house for ages. I mean the whole cast and spouses and the stage managers and the committee . . . Monsieur et Madame Boulton ne peuvent pas venir, Victorine, au moins ça veut dire deux personnes en moins . . . Et le vin blanc, c'est refroidi?'

'Non, Madame, j'ai chauffé le vin blanc, et refroidi le vin rouge.'

'Ah, Victorine, vous vous moquez de moi.'

'Tout est prêt, Madame, comme je vous ai promis.'

Henry tumbles through the door, happy and in mildly disreputable clothes suitable for a person of artistic temperament, followed by Betty.

'Henry, thank heavens you're back, so much to do – oh, Betty – how long do you think before all these people arrive? Will you go and look at the dining room to see if everything is as we want it?'

'I said to them, don't be too early. Helen, I do hope you really enjoyed the play, you weren't just being polite?'

'Darling, it was a triumph, you were ideal as David, so much yourself, so dry ... Henry, should we have some candles in here or is the electric lamp enough?'

Betty emerges from the dining room. It is perfectly in order.

'No seating plan, Henry darling, are you sure that's wise? It seems very Bohemian ...'

'We're all thespians this evening, you know – it's our natural habitat, a little unexpectedness and unconvention-ality ...'

'But this is Lou Paradou, we have a reputation to maintain – still, if you think no seating plan is all right ... Victorine – where is Victorine? I shall have to go and find her ... Darling, do you have enough clothes on? That jacket, the one you were wearing in the play, is very light, shouldn't you have a jersey too or at least a heavier jacket?'

She is about to exit (towards the kitchen) as the doorbell rings, but on hearing it turns instead to greet her guests. Margaret Lang (who has been playing Sorel) and Tom (Simon) enter. They are a young brother and sister, visiting their Mentone parents from London, who have been co-opted into the production. They were slightly under-rehearsed, some of the audience thought, but are nice-looking and lively. Like Henry, they are still wearing their stage clothes.

'Margaret, Tom, so very nice to see you both...'

'Oh, Mrs Williamson. It's so kind of you to have us, this great crowd of people...'

'Simply marvellous of you, Mrs Williamson. It's hard not to go on speaking in character, especially in this house which reminds one of the Blisses' house...' (*sotto voce*, to his sister) 'God, I'm dying for a drink, d'you think we'll get something quite soon? No sign of anything.'

'I thought you were both so good, so clever of you to fit into the production in such a short time. Are your parents coming to supper too?'

'Yes, they are if that's all right, we thought it would be too exciting for them but they insisted. How pretty the hall looks, Mrs Williamson.'

'I do wish you'd call me Helen. It does look nice, doesn't it? Will you have something to drink? Here's Victorine.'

Enter in a flood of chatter several groups, the rest of the cast, various attachments, the stage manager, two star-struck daughters of local families acting as assistant stage managers – but not the director. Francis deftly organises them, removes outer garments, ensures that they have something to drink, introduces them to his mother.

'Where's Vyvyan?'

'He was in a flap. He thought there should be a car to bring him here.'

'Won't he come? How unfortunate, should I telephone him at his hotel?'

'Oh, Monica's working on him. If she can't, no one... I'm sure he'll be here...'

'Darling you were divine. The end of Act Two was sensational.'

'Didn't you love the set? Wasn't the Williamsons' gramophone perfect?'

'So clever of Henry to do Simon's cartoons, they looked divine from the auditorium.'

'Won't you have a drink? I'm sure you need one.'

'You must be Francis Williamson, what a good host you are.'

'Veronica, or should I call you Clara, the voice was wonderful — how do you get it so right living down here? You can't have heard a genuine Cockney for years.'

'You'd be surprised, darling, some of the people here are more Cockney than meets the eye.'

Sensational moment as Monica, actress friend of the Williamsons from London, who has been playing Judith Bliss, makes a grand entrance with the producer. He is a faintly bad-tempered man also from London who has spent two weeks knocking his amateur company into shape and wishes he were working on something serious back home or even better in California.

'Wonderful production, we owe it all to you, such a success, I can't tell you, we've never done anything so good.'

He seems mollified. It is after all a very pretty house and the champagne helps and his hostess seems delighted to see him and insists that he must sit on her right.

Serving oneself and sitting down at little tables is an amusing innovation, don't you think, and so convenient. It was suggested by Francis who says it's quite the thing in London — Mulligatawny, one of those Indian specialities, so good at Lou Paradou! — Hot soup seemed essential, people might have caught a chill coming out of the casino into the cold street — I love the name, what can it mean? — Quick

Tom sit over there next to Francis, so sweet Francis isn't he, such an innocent look but... don't look to your right or we'll have to sit next to that dreary stage-manager person, he's waving at us, most familiar, just ignore him, get Francis to sit down — Wine, wine, is there no wine oh thank God — Mr Eliot, I'm so pleased to have you next to me, our guest of honour. It's all very plain food I'm afraid, only chicken salad, but the potatoes are called *gâteau de pommes de terre*, from Puerto Rico, which we think is nice, I hope you don't think it's lazy, a cold supper — Delighted, what pleasant people you have here in Menton. You must have been to enormous trouble moving furniture, what a huge room this is — My son Francis, just over there, pink face, was marvellous, worked on it all day with Franco, one of the gardeners, all I did was criticise and change my mind — What should the next play be? — Can you come and help us again it would be too divine? — Wasn't it too funny when Tom forgot his lines in the middle of Act Two and the prompter had gone to sleep I nearly died — I didn't forget my lines, only once — What's your next role in London, Monica? — Actually it's Manchester, but we hope London too, *The Circle*, Somerset Maugham, you know, very clever, about people abandoning conventional rules and fulfilling themselves emotionally, not enough of that around — It sounds daring, do you think we could play it in Mentone, a bit strong for the 'aunts' I would think — Hope they like *Hay Fever* — Are 'aunts' dying out, I think they must be, can't go on for ever or do they just reproduce themselves by some peculiar biological process? — Tom, shush! — You must come during the day, Mr Eliot, and see the garden though it's not looking very special at this time of year — This is such a pretty room, I think the

Williamsons have the nicest villa in Mentone, might almost be in England except for the weather.

Chatter and laughter become loud, the room grows warm, Tom wants to take off his jacket but his sister prevents him with stern look, leading lady flirts vivaciously with her host who responds pleasurably. Betty does not sit down but watches by the door to the butler's pantry and ensures that plates and glasses are never empty.

'Since it's so near Christmas we thought we'd have Christmas pudding which lots of people don't ever taste here, there's fruit salad too, it was difficult to persuade our cook to make plum pudding at first but when she'd done it once, she found it satisfying, or so she says.' (*Sotto voce*) 'Betty is everything under control do you know that girl Margaret Lang asked if she could be shown the geography, seems very forward to me but I suppose I'm old-fashioned ... d'you think I should take the ladies upstairs? I suppose after all that acting ...'

What are you doing for Christmas will you be at church or do you go to the Scottish one – Pity it's such a business getting to Italy these days we used to go to San Remo which has the nicest English church, not as busy as the one here, charming vicar – Margaret, how did she take your bold request, she obviously let you go? – I thought she looked a bit frosty, too absurd – I want some more to drink, angel, do you think I could ask that nice parlourmaid, drink seems a bit slow here – 'I've given you all that makes life worth living – my youth, my womanhood, and now my child. Would you tear the very heart out of me? ...' – Marvellous, I love that bit – Don't forget we've got four more nights, darling, don't tire yourselves out – No more fluffing from Tom, I hope –

Oh, shut up, Margaret – I want to see you all at the theatre tomorrow at three o'clock, a few technical problems, yes, everybody – It makes Henry so happy, but do you think he looks a bit flushed, has he over-exerted himself, Betty, what d'you think?

Finally they go, rather like birds migrating, all at once, leaving the family among the happy chaos. Briefly Helen consents to sit down and not worry.

'The play was a huge success Pa, I loved your performance, and the set looked marvellous, and Monica was delicious.'

'Thank you, Francis, well, I did my best, such a good role. The dinner was magnificent. Thank you, my darling, for arranging everything. Should we go and thank Madame Amélie?'

'I don't want you to get over-tired, Henry. Are you sure you won't, acting five nights in a row?'

'Shall we do our duty in the kitchen?'

The play was a great success. It was warmly reviewed in the *Menton and Monte Carlo News*, and attracted capacity audiences every night. As the Williamsons remarked to one another, it was consoling for once to have something cheerful to think about.

❧ JUNE 1938 ❧

ELEN AND HENRY had always spent most of the summer in England. They maintained the old-fashioned view that it was unhealthy for delicate people such as themselves to stay on the Riviera during the hot months. Besides, they disliked the heat, and they enjoyed going home. Until 1930 they kept Blithbury, the house in Staffordshire where Helen had grown up and where Aunt Susan had lived, but after her death this came into question. They discussed at length what to do, Helen wanting to keep the house where she had grown up and where she and Henry had courted (as she liked to say) and where the lakes and the little Chinese bridge and the tennis court under the cedar held pleasant memories. But, as Henry argued, they were only at Blithbury two or three months a year, and while their investments (her investments, but they always spoke, at her insistence, as though the money belonged to both of them) were holding up remarkably well, anyone relying on invested income must be careful – look at what had happened in Germany. Besides which, the day of the country house was passing, with even the richest families retrenching. Helen listened to Henry, unaware that he found staying at Blithbury uninteresting, and did not relish the role of temporary squire which the house conferred on him. She did not raise the matter for a few days, and he knew her well enough not to interrupt her thinking. One morning she announced that they must abandon the house, and then there was no more discussion. They did not renew the lease. After a year or two when nobody expressed any interest in taking it, the building was pulled down. The abandonment of the house and, still more, its demolition caused distress to Charles. He had regarded the place where he had spent his summer holidays since the age of eight as his own special home, where he and his aunt could play hide-and-seek and tennis, during long evenings when none of the rules of Lou Paradou applied. But as his father said to him, 'When you grow up you must find your own garden.'

So after 1930 they would stay in rented houses, or in hotels (these usually caused problems since Helen was used to standards higher than country hotels could offer), or with their faithful friends (who may not have found them the easiest of guests, since Helen expected without realising it that the effortless luxury of her own house would be easily attained by all her friends), or for the odd day or two in London. Helen, unlike Henry, hated London. She regarded it as the most unhealthy place in the world, and the idea of going to the London theatre, where the breath and clothing of several hundred people who had been moving for hours around the filthy metropolis were forced into unnatural closeness filled her with revulsion. She liked visiting the National Gallery but even there, there were so many people and many of them wore such dirty clothes . . .

On the whole they travelled together, using the devices for respecting each other's tastes developed over years. But sometimes, and particularly in later years, they would separate, she and her maid staying in a hotel in Brighton or

Eastbourne to enjoy the sea air and the atmosphere of gentility, which she found faintly absurd but reassuring, he visiting his sons or seeking out obscure historical monuments that had caught his fancy in his previous year's reading. By the late 1930s it had become the custom for him to spend a few days each year with Charles in London. These were happy times, when Henry and Charles talked like brothers, like contemporaries, without constraint.

The last visit of this sort took place in June 1938. It lasted only a few days, too few. As Henry thought to himself as he left, 'Why do we organise our lives so that the happy days are surrounded by years of dutiful frustration? Why are we so ruled by convention?' For these few days he was indeed freed. Charles had moved into a new flat in Bloomsbury, which though not large had a garden and a fine eighteenth-century room on the street. His father slept in a tiny spare room, which was intended for use as the study – 'But it will always be cleared when you come to visit, as you often will,' said Charles expansively. Standing at the door, looking at the minute proportions of the room and the narrow bed, with much of the space taken up by the large Baroque carving of a saint which Charles had just bought (for no money at all, he assured his father), they found themselves exchanging a smile. This was not a room where Mrs Henry Williamson would care to sleep.

During their week together, they painted the whole flat – as Charles put it, decorators never achieved what one wanted. 'You don't mind being treated as cheap labour, do you, Pa?' he said jocularly to his father, who replied that indeed he didn't, it was nice to be useful. Anne would come round in the evening and tell them about the day's inexhaustibly entertaining events (as she made them sound) at her publishing house. They would sit in the garden while Charles explained how he intended to re-create Lou Paradou in miniature and on English lines, drinking white wine out of the old glasses he collected. One evening they took a picnic to Regent's Park, but generally they went round the corner to a little restaurant where you could have dinner for half a crown, or to Charlotte Street, and talked and talked, With much teasing, Charles and Anne persuaded Henry to go out for dinner without a tie. They tried to get him not to wear a hat in the street, but failed on that one.

One day a package arrived from Eastbourne, addressed to Henry, with large familiar lettering on the outside announcing 'URGENT — HANDLE WITH CARE'. Henry eyed it without enthusiasm and found inside three jerseys and a note from his wife to say that she thought that the weather was uncertain (it had been over eighty degrees for a week) and that he ought to have these garments to hand in case of inclemency. He showed the jerseys to Charles. Charles looked at them incredulously, caught his father's eye, and burst into laughter, seizing one, crying, 'I'm so cold,' and rolling with the thick green wool over his head on to the sofa. His father laughed too, but not for so long, and not so hard, and after a while said, 'Enough, Charles.' His son stood up, looked his father in the eye, and laid his hand on his father's arm.

By the end of the week the flat had been completely repainted. With delicate tones of ivory in the front room and subtle green in the bedroom, it looked, as Charles remarked, 'as elegant as anyone could hope for — though it won't stay that way long'. As they drank their vermouth that evening ('Where on earth did you get this disgusting stuff? Bad enough to have to drink it in France,' as Henry remarked) Charles said to Anne, 'Pa has been wonderful, helping me with all this. You wouldn't believe how hard he has worked, and hardly an hour off to go and look at things.' 'I've enjoyed it so much,' said his father. 'It's been so wonderful to be allowed to get one's hands dirty for once, without being scolded.'

⊰ FEBRUARY 1939 ⊱

T HEY WERE LATE FOR TEA. Definitely, and after a while dreadfully, late. She would not have minded if they had made it clear when they set off after lunch that they were going to miss tea. But no, Charles had said in his most airy way, 'Don't worry, Ma, we'll be back at half past four without fail, I only want to show Anne the Old Town at Ventimiglia and maybe those extraordinary Baroque gates to vanished villas at Latte and we might possibly look into La Mortola for two minutes. I suppose we can get in even if it's closed, you know the Hanburys a bit, don't you?' Henry had murmured about packing in too much, knowing that Charles had inherited from both his parents a passion for sightseeing, which was incompatible with punctuality. But he was unwilling to scold Charles, for whom he felt a hardly defined compassion, and kept saying to Helen that he was a grown man, must be allowed to go his own way, as though Charles were capable of looking after himself sensibly. So here they were, she and Henry and Betty, sitting in the drawing room with piles of tea, sandwiches and bread and butter and sponge cake and all the rest over which Madame Amélie had taken such trouble. There was a limit to how much the three of them could eat, indeed she could scarcely eat at all. Half past four meant half past four, as Charles knew, and she was disappointed that Anne, such a nice and sensible girl, had not obliged him to be more reliable. It was all very well, being so artistic — but sometimes one had to think about the details of life, and other people's convenience as well as one's own.

They sat over tea for almost an hour. Helen was annoyed at the start of the little ceremony, and as the minutes passed her irritation increased. She showed her mood by harassing her companions with worries about day-to-day matters. Had Betty arranged the tickets for the opera in Monte Carlo, and had Henry written to the Army and Navy Stores about the new china they needed, and why was the drive up to the house so badly swept these days and was the gardener getting too old, and mingled with all this were comments, repeated yet developing, about the tea being spoilt and whether they would order another pot when the children did come back and what would they do with all the food and sometimes she found time to worry where on earth Charles and Anne were and whether they had had a car accident or been arrested or since Charles was so vague perhaps they had fallen over the side of the mountain or just driven off to San Remo to look at some altarpiece he had just remembered. Her husband and Betty knew that in this mood there was hardly any pacifying her. Lately they had found that jokes they had been used to making and habitual affectionate and consoling gestures — he would stroke her neck, or lay his hand gently on the side of her head — were less effective in making her smile, or calming her. They must wait for the mood to blow over. Usually it did, with the help of a little migraine and a withdrawal to her room.

At half past five the tea was removed. The disappearance of this apparatus of civility made the situation worse. Helen took to pacing round the room, tidying up the books and magazines in a convulsive way. Betty and Henry exchanged glances and Betty left the room. She had, after all, other things to do, and they knew that Henry was often better at soothing Helen by himself. They had, indeed, a mute programme for managing her, which quite often succeeded and at least prevented her from succumbing to desperation. In the noisy silence that followed, Henry suggested that he should ring the police to report that the young people had not returned from a visit to Italy. The police were unable to help. He proposed that they should walk into the garden and examine their new plants, reminded his wife that they had the vaguest son in the world and put his arm round her shoulders. Then he looked into her face and saw there an expression of frightened sadness, which he could hardly hope to dispel. He felt, himself, a moment of desperation.

At a quarter to seven, in the twilight, the car drove up to the front door. Charles and Anne emerged. Before they had time to move up the principal stairs, Helen threw open the heavy glass front door and raged towards them. 'Where have you been?' she cried. 'You're late for tea, you've ruined the afternoon, you're almost late for dinner, you said you would be back at half past four, we've been so worried, it's so rude and thoughtless, where on earth have you been, it's no good saying you've been delayed by this or that, you've just been amusing yourselves in Italy...'

Charles looked pale and angry and obstinate and stared at his mother in silence. Anne, also pale, was the one who spoke.

'I'm extremely sorry,' she said. 'You must put the blame on me. I insisted that I wanted to walk in the mountains on the Italian side, because I had never seen them. I'm afraid we took the wrong path, and — and we were arrested.'

'Arrested!' cried Helen and Henry simultaneously.

'Yes' she said. 'By the Italian border guards. We were wandering along what seemed a perfectly normal path — there was a sign saying admission was forbidden but we ignored it . . .'

'Ridiculous that sort of sign,' interjected Charles. 'Why shouldn't we walk along a very pretty mountain path if we want to?'

'And suddenly two men in uniform appeared round the corner and . . . and . . .' She stopped, as though remembering the moment.

'And they pointed guns at us,' Charles finished the sentence for her.

'Guns!' cried Helen.

'They told us we were under arrest,' said Anne, 'and this was a forbidden zone open only to authorised persons and we were committing a serious offence and where were our papers? Fortunately we had our passports. When they saw we were English and that Charles's address was given as Mentone they changed a bit, but they weren't more friendly, not at all. They made us get into the car and took us to a police station, next to the frontier.'

'Oh God,' said Helen. 'You'd better come into the house.'

Victorine appeared, wondering if they would like tea. 'No, no, they can't have tea,' said her mistress, and led them into the drawing room.

'And what happened there?' asked Henry. 'Surely they didn't keep you? Didn't you tell them to telephone the vice-consul in San Remo, or to telephone us?'

'They put us into a room and kept us waiting for a while. And then they asked us endlessly about what we had been doing and were we spying and didn't we realise what frontiers meant. And one of them who was more educated and spoke French said that in future there would be no problems over the frontier here because Mentone was an Italian town and soon it would belong to Italy again and...' She stopped herself.

'And what, Anne?' asked Helen.

'That was all.'

'No,' said Charles, 'that was not all. He said, "Your family..." Just that, and then he shrugged his shoulders, and smiled in a knowing sort of way.'

'Oh, never mind that, it doesn't mean anything,' said Henry hastily. 'Just bravado. How long did they keep you?'

'About an hour,' said Anne. 'It was horrible. I've never been in a place where I felt so threatened. There was an atmosphere of menace and hostility, all those stupid brutish-looking men in uniforms, no women anywhere, that made it worse.'

'And how did you get away?'

'We both had to fill in a form,' said Charles, 'and then we asked to see the British consul and they said that would not be necessary since we could leave. But they told us to be very careful next time we visited Italy, since Italy was not a place for making mistakes in. They'd brought our car down from the mountain, so we drove back over the border.'

Anne burst violently into tears. Faced with this, Helen melted and put her arms round her.

'It was an interesting experience, I suppose,' said Charles, beginning to rally himself. 'Direct experience of the Fascists on the receiving end, as it were. If we had gone a little further, I suppose we might have seen the gun emplacements on the frontier, the ones people speak about so much, with the guns directed at France.'

His father looked him in the eye, then glanced significantly at Helen and back at Charles.

The walk and the arrest were not discussed again.

⊰ APRIL 1939 ⊱

IN A SENSE they were repeating the usual pattern of going away in the early summer. They had never stayed in Mentone during the summer. It was true that this year they would not, as usual, be travelling to England. Equally, touring Italy or Austria, as they had often done in the past, was hardly appropriate now. If one thought about it (and it was better not to) hostile countries seemed to be massed around their bastion of France. They could visit the Netherlands, Helen speculated to Henry, or see some French cathedrals or go to the châteaux of the Loire where they had not been for some time... He thought they were better settling down in Pau.

What was unusual, this time, was that they were closing up Lou Paradou. Not permanently, of course, but probably for a good while. This operation allowed some exercise for Henry's underused powers of organisation. They made a detailed tour of the house, with Betty acting as scribe and adviser, to inspect and list everything it contained. This took several days. Though it was a melancholy experience, they quite enjoyed it. They appreciated the feeling of purpose it gave them, the lists and categories and discussions. They even relished the dreamlike sense of viewing their past lives as in a panorama, through the books and chairs and mementoes they had accumulated over so many years but usually hardly noticed. As they looked at the marble carving of a cherub's head which they had bought, they seemed to remember, in Gubbio in 1924 (it was indeed 1924, Henry later found, seeking confirmation in the photograph albums), Helen said in surprise, 'Henry, we've had so many happy times together, haven't we? We've had so much fun, lovey darling.' She used the phrase of their early marriage, which she had seldom spoken recently. 'Yes, dearest,' he said briskly, more interested in pursuing the work in hand.

They divided the contents of the house into several categories. Some things they must take to Pau. The Villa Hirondelle, which they had rented for two years, was a furnished house, over-furnished in fact, but many of their possessions they could not bring themselves to leave behind: some of their most precious books, a favourite set of wine glasses, the Royal Worcester porcelain, the visitors' book. The most valuable objects they were sending to the owner of a furniture depot in Tours, who had looked after things for them before and would protect anything they consigned to him. Into this category went the watercolours, the Napoleonic table with the portraits in enamel of the marshals, the Chippendale dining-room chairs ('But do you know, darling, Charles said he thought these might be Victorian . . . What do you think of that? Not Chippendale or Georgian at all?'), the two carved French chairs, an Italian mirror. The third group included everything they were to leave in the house, most of the larger furniture, most of the books, the portrait of Helen as a girl (which they stored in the attic, wrapped up, hoping it would be safe), the domestic apparatus accumulated over twenty-five years, the contents of the servants' rooms, the gay and optimistic furnishings of the spare room, which had charmed so many guests. With care they chose presents for the servants, inviting them to select what they wanted. When the servants modestly held back, Helen and Henry found for them silver bowls and Meissen figures and photographs, objects that could be easily transported to Belgium and Switzerland. All the servants were dispersing; only Victorine was staying with them. She refused to take refuge with her family and had made it clear to her old mother in Castellar that she had several other sons and daughters and grandchildren to look after her and could very well manage without Victorine, who had other responsibilities. And of course there was Betty, who would not for a moment consider going back to Scotland. Betty would surely remain with them till the end.

'It may be only for a short time that we part,' Helen said to Emma. They were engaged in the morning toilette, and Emma was giving her mistress occasional advice, in case an experienced lady's maid was not to be found in Pau in these unsettled times. 'All this trouble may just end, and Herr Hitler may see reason and realise that he has enough to look after at home. Quite soon, everything may be normal again.' And Emma smiled, wondering to herself whether Belgium would again be invaded in the way she remembered from her girlhood. But both knew, though they never said it, that once they had said goodbye . . .

Pau seemed the obvious place to move to while life risked being complicated at home. Pleasant houses, pretty countryside, large English community, all the advantages of such a community, no shortage of home comforts one always needs, French shops not good, close to Pyrenees and in case of crisis it would be easy or at least not too hard to escape, that was too dramatic, to leave France over the Spanish border or by boat. Free of the anxiety of Italy so close. They had no trouble finding a house, books of house agents in Pau groaned with villas for rent, large and small, as though Pau were no longer a place people sought out. Many of them owned or rented by British families where had they gone all those comfortable people there had even been a fox hunt in Pau at one time where had it gone

the spring season in Mentone had been very muted usual events were organised English church kept services going tennis club had its Easter party but Menton Players after its Christmas season was not making any more plans, some people had not come back this year without properly explaining why not the Rentons for example who had been coming since the Great War but some people were staying on some believed like many of the French apparently that Hitler would never dare to attack France and the Maginot Line was invincible wasn't it

motored over to Pau at the beginning of the year and looked around the town, viewing possible houses only a few. Without difficulty, they settled on a house standing among many other villas in a handsome residential suburb, very different from Lou Paradou, more like England, thick hedges and shrubs around the edge of the garden and a large lawn in front of the house, rather unkempt but once fine, in shaggy French lawn way, curving gravel paths, grey French gravel not pretty at all, a large gravelled space in front of the house which was relatively new, probably from the turn of the century. Unlike Lou Paradou, this house was built of grey stone with a sloping tiled roof, more Atlantic than Mediterranean as Henry remarked as they stood outside it had all they needed, a pretty drawing room looking on to the garden, a dining-room convenient for the kitchen, a little room that could be used as a study or a private sitting room, an unimpressive staircase but who was there to be impressed, four bedrooms on the first floor, several little bedrooms above. It was not glamorous not as large or beautiful as their own house but that was not to be expected and, as Henry would remark, they would not be here for long and no doubt they could soon go back to Mentone or perhaps even to England, making it all sound so calm and easy and pleasant. But in reality the choices were not so easy and she would not respond, would change the subject, talk of carpets and whether they should bring curtains from home since the ones in the villa were so mean her mind feverish would turn over the horror of the alternatives, England at war, England invaded, the fear of what might happen if Germany

Fun, Henry said, to create a new household again. The quantity of furniture already at the house limited what they could do but with some judicious weeding they could make it look all right it was mostly French about twenty or thirty years old perfectly acceptable though *triste* muted colours highly polished once but dusty now, but they would bring over some things from home and buy necessities in Pau, easy since people were always moving house but why they were always moving they were not told

They sorted out who had which room. On the first floor, Helen, Henry, Betty, spare. Victorine upstairs. They would find a new cook in Pau. As for a lady's maid, they would be living simply and probably Betty and Victorine could help her though what did it matter now how she looked or was dressed it was irrelevant they would hardly be seeing society

some of the furniture from Lou Paradou would look nice there but it was not sensible Henry kept saying to her when she suggested or even begged to include one or two more precious things in their load to bring over too much such things easily found in Pau if not quite the same but some of the pictures had to come though not her portrait which was extremely large and might be damaged in transit and some other reminders of home some favourite pieces of furniture this was not a barracks they were moving to not an internment camp not a prison but a home keeping up the idea of home was so important and Francis would come and visit them and other friends who would come who would risk coming

she must not give way to dark thoughts she must stay calm she must be organised she must be

cupboards how little she had thrown away, clothes for tennis parties in the 1910s, clothes worn for the hospital in the Great War, evening dresses from the 1920s. How absurd they looked now though there was nothing from the time before Mentone how could these things be made useful to someone would there be a jumble sale at the church would the vicar be staying

They motored over several times to Pau. By the end of April the new house seemed almost ready. 'You have made it look so like home,' Henry said. It was so kind of him, he was so appreciative when one made an effort though not always as ready to show his affection as she would like. – Do you remember, she said to him, the first day we viewed Lou Paradou such a happy day my darling and we both knew at once didn't we that it was the house for us didn't we my darling? she said again since he did not reply at once

In May the Germans entered Prague

At the beginning of that month, Helen and Henry made their final preliminary visit to the Villa Hirondelle. It was perfectly in order. They could not delay their move any longer nor did it seem wise to. When they returned to Mentone, they found their house strangely quiet and tidy. The best furniture had been sent away and there should have been gaps everywhere, but someone had rearranged the remaining furniture and filled the rooms with flowers so that for the last few days the house should not seem empty or bleak. With more force then ever before, they realised how much they had accumulated over the years, filling the rooms with trophies of their lives and friendships, trophies which now hardly signified. – It looks so clean and fresh doesn't it my darling, so modern, said Henry, and after all when we come back we can start to collect things again

They did not want to leave the house looking as though it were uninhabited even though it would be. Henry spoke to a house agent about the possibility of letting the house for a while but the agent laughed and said he did not think he could find anybody at this moment who would be interested indeed he had to admit that after thirty years he was intending to close his business and retire to somewhere near Bordeaux where his wife had family

Betty would come with them Betty would come with them Betty would come with them that was the great solace but how far would she come would she stay with them till the end lately she had seemed abstracted, withdrawn, had started reading old letters and talking almost as though she did not realise what she was doing about her youth in Scotland and the pleasure of going back now

servants would stay until they had left and then disperse – Franco would remain and look after the garden and keep an eye on everything live in the gardener's house at the top of the garden and they would go on paying him, pay him that is as long as transferring money around Europe and out of England

On their last afternoon at Lou Paradou, Mr and Mrs Williamson walked through the house together. It was a hot day, the sun no less brilliant than ever. No dust sheets yet, but dust sheets hung, as it were, in the air. The shutters were closed in the rooms, many of which seemed already to have fallen asleep. They had not used the drawing room for some weeks, they had not had the heart to sit there and they had hardly had any guests recently. The chandelier had gone, and most of the furniture. The space no longer seemed theirs. The boys' rooms and the spare room had long since been tidied and emptied of contents other than larger pieces of furniture. Since Francis was still unmarried (so was Charles, as Henry pointed out, but after all Charles had made a life for himself elsewhere and was out of the nest in a way darling Francis was not) Helen preferred to take some of his possessions with them to Pau, a pair of pyjamas, a paper knife he had had as a child, one or two of his favourite books; he would certainly visit them and would like to see something of his own in their new house. In their own rooms life flickered on, but it was a life, they knew, that was effectively over. Their suitcases were packed, the rooms after the chaos of the past few days were orderly, the flowers arranged with loving thoughtfulness for their brief return were beginning to droop. In the spare room Henry opened the shutters so that their bodies were suffused by the heat of the sun and their eyes dazzled again by the sparkle of the sea. 'We shall not see the sea in Pau,' she said. 'We must say goodbye to the sea. You know, my darling, we always meant to take a boat to Corsica, but we never went, did we?'

'We'll go when we come back,' he said. 'You know, dearest, we mustn't assume that we will not return to Mentone. There may be no war in France, it may all be sorted out peacefully.'

'Do you remember, Henry,' she said, 'when we first visited the house, how magical it seemed, how we wandered through these empty rooms, they had no associations for us then, did they, they seemed full of promise and hope, and only twenty-seven years have passed, such a short time, and now we're old, and nobody needs us and it's all finished . . .'

'Helen,' he replied, 'my love, don't talk like that. It's not true what you say, and it's so painful to hear such words, and what can anyone say in response?'

'I'm sorry,' she said, 'but it's painful to suffer these experiences. Life is full of pain, nothing but pain, until finally death . . .'

'Won't you take comfort in the sea?' he asked her, gesturing from the window towards the huge shining prospect. 'You've always loved the sea, it's always consoled you.'

'We're leaving the sea, Henry,' she answered. 'There's no sea at Pau, only the mountains, those huge mountains, much bigger than Le Berceau. We should go and look at that beastly Berceau, I think, one last time.'

The garden was celebrating the spring with particular vigour that year, or so it seemed to Henry and Helen. The irises, mauve along one terrace, white along the terrace below, were standing in perfect order; the judas tree, magnificently pink, was in full flower in the wild garden among the ancient olive trees; behind the house, the orange trees exulted in their blossom. On the top terrace under the lofty ivy-clad wall, which concealed the houses of their neighbours, sheltered the rows of sweet peas which grew here as never in England. The garden was being tended as lovingly as ever, and Franco had no intention of neglecting it. They would have known this even if he had not told them so. But tell them he did as they finally left, standing at the front door with a bouquet of sweet peas tied with pink ribbon, and bringing them as close to tears as they allowed themselves to be, on that melancholy day of departure.

Pau has a population of 35,000. It has three English churches and a Scottish church; two English physicians, and three clubs including an English club; golf links and a lawn tennis club; an English Reading Room and a Circulating Library. Fox-hunting (four times a week in the season), fishing and shooting, can be enjoyed. It is a handsome town, one of the most frequented and favourite winter resorts in France, with a large English colony. The season lasts from the beginning of November to the end of May. The town authorities have spent large sums on improving and beautifying promenades and drives. On the two-mile Boulevard des Pyrénées rise most of the principal hotels. The climate is sedative and beneficial to nervous and irritable temperaments. Chest complaints, bronchitis, and rheumatism are also benefited, and the town is sheltered from the south and west winds. The Place Royale at the southern extremity of the town, with a statue of Henry IV standing in the centre, commands magnificent views. The Parc National or Grand Parc lies at the west of the town, at the extremity of which commences the Plaine de Billère, where the English colony and visitors have established their various games and clubs. There are numerous promenades and excursions in the vicinity.

(ADAPTED FROM THOMAS COOK AND SON, *The Travellers' Handbook for the Riviera*, 1912)

⇻≈ 12 JUNE 1939 ≈⇺

Letter from Charles Williamson to Anne Smith

Villa Hirondelle, Pau,
12 June 1939

Dearest A

I have been here now for two days and I wish you were
here too. The parents have moved into their new house
and seem determined to be pleased with it. It's smallish
and ugly compared to Lou Paradou but I suppose it passes
as a respectable house in Pau terms. Quite a large garden
but surrounded by other similar bourgeois houses, mostly
rather unattractive too. They have been very busy making
it homelike. I suppose I find this a bit pathetic since this
place is so clearly not home, just a rented house, a shelter
from the Fascist blast. It's full of mediocre furniture and
some terrible French Victorian prints of cows and merry
peasants and even awful bits of religious stuff here and
there, left over from the owners, which it seems impious to
burn (though tempting). The house had been empty for a
while and when they arrived apparently it smelt a bit but
that has been dealt with by the devoted if depleted staff.
Attacking the garden has been a major enterprise and
they've been busy getting the lawn cut, Pa very active in
this and Ma seems for once not determined to stop him
exerting himself. They're anxious to make the best of

everything. Driving round the countryside seeing places they've never visited before is a major excitement. They're still busy taking photographs and sticking them into albums, which I suppose is a statement of confidence.

They seem all right, quite cheerful. Whether that's just moral courage and stiff upper lip and all the rest of it I don't know. No complaints on their part, no regrets expressed for Lou Paradou which was after all the centre of their life for nearly thirty years. I wish I understood them. I wish I understood anything. It all seems more complicated and hopeless the older one gets. I'm so depressed about being thirty, not young any more. Haven't achieved anything.

I'm sorry we had such a bad evening the other day. I know I'm hopeless in some ways, I know I don't show enough affection, I know you must find me frustrating. But that's just me, I'm afraid. Do you love me? Do I love you? What do these old words mean? Aren't we at the stage of understanding that 'love' as it's called is the result of temporary physical attraction based on an idealised view of the other person, generally stimulated by the need to satisfy some psychological inadequacy in oneself? Can we still allow ourselves these outmoded elixirs, which seem to be a means of preventing people from expressing themselves in more socially disruptive ways? Anyway, if one has been brought up to repress one's emotions it's hard to believe in the mystique of midsummer night's dream. I'm convinced that in childhood one's natural feelings were suppressed both by the parents – who never ever talk, or talked, about their real feelings or their quite complicated relationship – and by school, where one was trained to repress emotion. The masters, the boys, they all did it – not brutally, but by endless ribbing, and irony as one got older. It was all pretty effective, made one hide one's feelings, pretend to be tough or cynical or whatever.

Reading that again, it doesn't sound very affectionate – but you know what I'm getting at. You're a very special person but I'm just not sure that I can give you what you need. Can I?

I could go on at length about poor old Ma and Pa but won't bore you too much with that subject. As I say, creating a new system of comfort in Pau seems to be the principal objective as though they were going to be here for years. Anyway, the household functions here much as before if rather reduced, Betty still in charge, the food – which as you know is Ma's passion – is ample and pretty good, they've found some shops they like, they've made one or two friends of the solid Mentone type and are able to get up bridge fours, the countryside is extremely pretty. And of course Spain is near – if anyone wants to go to Spain these days – and the boat service from Bordeaux to England is reliable, at the moment anyway.

The only problem, of course, is that as far as one knows Armageddon lies round the corner, just beyond the next comfortable villa. That's not so easy to deal with. Efficient lawn mowing and pretty lampshades won't deter the Panzers.

Seriously, I just don't know what to expect and hope for, as far as they're concerned. I can't help worrying. But at least they're happy for the moment, or a bit happy, or pretending to be happy.

As for us – I do love you, you know, old thing. I'm

sorry to be so difficult about it. Love and marriage and all of that are pretty wonderful, I know. It's just that when I see them in operation, as I do here, it all seems so difficult, so sad really, so inhibiting. But I suppose stable relationships don't have to be like that, do they?

See you soon.

Love

Charles

F RANCIS HAD ALWAYS been punctual, and when he was visiting his parents was even more so. Life at the Ministry had not made him any calmer about time — as he said himself, many of his colleagues spent more time worrying about keeping time than they did about what they were using the time for. As he and Lucy walked around Pau on their first afternoon there, to look for cheeses and *charcuterie* which they could take home and a wedding present which the parents could give them while they were close at hand, a sense of urgency was created by his unobtrusive but regular consultation of his watch. As the afternoon passed, this became more frequent, as he began to mutter exhortations such as 'Do come on, darling, we really don't have so much time.' Lucy took this uncomplainingly. Well, she thought, I'll be able to calm him down eventually, but while he's here and in these peculiar circumstances...

They found no wedding present that afternoon. Mrs Williamson had suggested that they might like to find something antique, 'something that would remind you of us,' she said with a laugh. But none of the *antiquaires* they visited had anything suitable for the little house in Chelsea they were moving into, everything was much too French or too large. Some of the shops had received quantities of furniture in bulk recently but none of this appealed to them.

Perhaps they could buy something new instead, such as an attractive dinner service ... though it looked dangerously as though they might be offered the ancestral service (dating back to at least 1880) if they said too much on that front.

When they arrived back at the villa, flushed and anxious, a quarter of an hour before the official hour for tea, Mrs Williamson appeared faintly bemused at their punctuality. She seemed, these days, not to mind so much about time – just as the famous *jour de repos* about which Lucy had heard from various sources had become occasional rather than weekly. All of this surprised Lucy who hardly knew her but had been told (not by Francis, who seldom said anything critical about anyone, especially not his mother) about her obsessiveness on this point. 'Oh, there should be some tea some time,' Mrs Williamson said, 'but since we've been here meal-times have become rather vague, not like the old days at all. Our new cook is not quite as organised as dear Madame Amélie in Mentone. It makes Victorine very cross but I don't know that it really matters. When the world's collapsing, what does a collapsed soufflé matter ...?' A tentative and oddly vague smile accompanied this remark.

She showed them into the drawing room, where a table had been covered with a white cloth. The room had recently been repainted and the curtains, though not new, were very pretty, green silk – 'We brought them from the Mentone house,' said Mrs Williamson, 'we were so pleased that they fitted these windows. I suppose in due course we might get some new ones. What d'you think, should we?' Tea appeared almost instantly. Surveying the table and its array of little plates and dishes with some complacency, she went on, 'Since we came here, Victorine has persuaded us that French cakes — we never used to eat them in Mentone, you know — are actually very good. There's the most delicious *pâtisserie* in the town, lots of English people go there, and they deliver. I've become quite a connoisseur of the French cake, particularly something called the *diplomate*, which is made with chestnut and cream, quite delicious . . .' Her figure confirmed this new connoisseurship.

No, they had not found the ideal wedding present, in spite of looking hard. 'If we were still living at home,' Mrs Williamson said, 'we could find you something we'd know you'd like, but as you see we're depleted of possessions in this house. But of course there's the old dinner service which we never use now, the one that came from my father. I couldn't bear to leave it behind at Mentone, though Henry said it was too large to bring here and we never used it much at Lou Paradou. It's very handsome, though a bit old-fashioned, I suppose. D'you think you'd like it?'

They made polite noises of enthusiasm. The conversation was moved on to their new house, the wedding. April 1940, it was to be, at St Columba's, Pont Street, with the reception at a house in Cadogan Square. They talked with regret about Charles, and the fact that after so many years Anne had broken off their friendship. Charles had not been at all forthcoming about this. 'I don't see Anne any more,' he merely muttered.

They did not discuss the political situation. Would any of them, they wondered tacitly, actually be in London in April? Would the church exist, or Cadogan Square? Would London have been bombed into non-existence? Would they exist themselves? Was it worthwhile making plans in one's head, and considering when one would come over to

England, and how long ahead, and where they'd stay . . .?

Tea was lavish, tea was almost engrossing, tea excluded the panic that threatened outside. And since they were staying in Pau for all of ten days, it seemed a good idea to make plans for excursions in the vicinity, and arrange a little party to meet some of the new friends. Ten days offered so many possibilities.

'There are some very nice people here, you know,' said Mrs Williamson. 'Many of them have been here for years. Did you know there was a fox hunt here until very recently, mostly English people but quite a few French as well? And an English Club, and a pretty good library. We find it very pleasant and it's fun to be able to visit new places, we'd seen everything near Mentone so often, nice as it all was. We think we shall enjoy life here very much . . .' As she made this optimistic prognosis a strange look, determined, wide-eyed, almost visionary, appeared on her face.

Through closed bedroom doors Lucy could hear the news on the wireless, several times a day.

At the end of the ten days, they all stood on the steps of the house to say goodbye. It had been a very pleasant visit, Lucy reflected, as they stood in a row to be photographed, smiling at the camera as though nothing disturbed their tranquillity. They had seen a great many churches and the outside of a great many châteaux, and explored the country-side, and made an expedition into the Pyrenees, and eaten an extraordinary amount as though tomorrow there might be nothing to eat, and talked about the old days at Mentone (where she had never been) and the new days at Pau. They had spoken hardly at all about the political situation and Czechoslovakia and Poland. The weather was hot, sunny, delicious. When Lucy woke each morning in her bright room she felt suffused with comfort and repose, feeling rather than seeing the sun spearing through the curtains. Then she would remember the political situation, and the foreboding, which seemed to her to have overshadowed all her adult life, would begin to ache again.

As they made their goodbyes, an order of precedence emerged. Lucy first kissed her future father-in-law, and then her future mother-in law. Both hugged her fondly – the visit had been a success. It was clear they thought Francis had chosen well. Francis was gripped round the shoulders by his father, who said, 'Goodbye, old boy. Thank you so much for coming out, it's been so important. And we're looking forward to the wedding. I suppose I shall have to get my morning coat let out, haven't worn it for years.' Then Francis embraced his mother. 'Goodbye, Ma,' he said. 'Goodbye, my darling mother. Next time we see you will probably be at the wedding, and I'm sure there'll be a big party before that, so you must come in good time and with your clothes and especially your hat all sorted out in advance.' She clung to him, her favourite child, the person to whose successful upbringing she felt she had indeed contributed though she had achieved so little else, the person who loved and comforted her without reserve. She clung, knowing that he, like everything else, would be taken away. Would they meet again, ever?

Her head on his shoulder, she whispered, 'Goodbye, my darling. I love you so much.' But he hardly heard, since her mouth was pressed against the cloth of his coat, and she could hardly articulate a word. Part of his mind was thinking that it would be simpler if they left before she burst into tears.

So they departed rather fast, driving rapidly away with many (but not too many) waves of the hand, his jaunty little sports car filled with their luggage and a Bayonne ham and cheeses (which they had had no trouble in finding) and an extremely pretty vase and the family dinner service, which they did not want but which clearly it was their mission to save. Francis could not face turning to wave a last goodbye, so Lucy looked back on his behalf as they were driving out though the front gate. She saw them still standing on the steps. Henry was waving at them resolutely, but Helen waved no more, her head pressed against her husband's shoulder; she seemed to be moving her hands but not as a gesture of farewell, and she looked, Lucy could not help noticing, less well than she had seemed in the past few days of vivacious hospitality.

Francis drove rather fast and in silence for an hour. And then, it being a beautiful day and the roads being clear, and since he could drive as fast as he liked and Lucy was beside him, his spirits seemed to rise. He gave her that smile, shy and tender and unafraid, which eventually had won the day for him as far as she was concerned, and said, 'Well, I don't know about you, darling, but I'm looking forward to my lunch...'

⊰ SEPTEMBER 1939 ⊱

'SO WHAT DOES THIS MEAN? Oh Henry, what terrible times we live in. Don't you remember, when we were young, how peaceful and easy life seemed? Everything was so secure, and now it's . . .'

'I don't know what this means. The Germans are very strong, but I'm sure we were right to say, "Enough is enough". Even if it means the destruction of our country.'

'The destruction? Darling, you shouldn't speak like that. I mean, the children . . . What will become of the children?'

'I suppose the Germans may bomb London tomorrow, or tonight, and for all I know destroy it in a few raids. Their bombs are so powerful, and our defences are so weak. Poor old London, I was fond of it once. Not much hope for London now.'

'The children . . . ?'

'The children aren't children now. They must look after themselves, they're quite old enough. Anyway, I doubt they'll be in London for long.'

'Perhaps Herr Hitler won't want to go on.'

'Hitler's a monster. He'll go on until he destroys Britain, and France, and perhaps all Europe. He has appetite for the fight, all right. The trouble is, I don't think we do. I don't believe the British, who've become so sleepy and fond of peace – us included, I suppose – will have the stomach to stand up to him. I can't see Britain fighting an enemy like this one.'

'Darling, what will happen to us? Darling, I can't go back to England, I can't face the journey, I can't face the danger or the difficulties when we get there. It may be invaded, and what would happen then? Darling, what are we to do?'

'We must wait and see what happens. There's always a reason to hope, I suppose. If you want to stay here, then that's what we must do.'

'What sort of hope, Henry? What hope can there be?'

'We must think of Frances, our poor refugee friend, and look after her. We must try to help her to get away, if that's what she wants. We must live in the moment, I suppose...'

'Henry, you're so kind and brave. But I can't... I can't...'

'Helen, you must do your best. You must try to do your best. I know you will. *Sang froid*, you know, stiff upper lip...'

'So we can stay here?'

'Yes, Helen, we can stay here. Stay till the end, if necessary.'

'The end? What end?'

'The end, whatever it may be.'

⊰ AUTUMN 1939 – SPRING 1940 ⊱

F OR THE WILLIAMSONS, as for many other people – that is to say, those who were not being arrested or killed – the autumn of 1939 was a time of nervous relaxation. As no invasion of France or the Netherlands took place, they allowed themselves to take comfort in their newly developed routine. Money was still coming through from their English bank. Procuring the necessities of life was not difficult. They became obscurely fond of the house, continuing to make modest improvements and suppressing doubts about the sense in doing this. They listened to the BBC news twice a day: this became a little ceremony, as satisfying as morning and evening prayers for their forebears. Betty, with less to do than she had had in Mentone, became they thought rather silent, not exactly brooding but contemplative, and spoke from time to time of her family in Aberdeen, and of her nephew who had joined the Navy. They all allowed themselves the hope that the situation might not be as black as it seemed, that Hitler might find the massed power of France and Britain more formidable than he had expected, that peace would prevail, and that they would be able to go home again to the shuttered house in Mentone. At any rate, thank God, Italy had remained neutral, and the Maginot Line surely provided a safe defence?

It was a quiet life physically. It was not a quiet life mentally, but less troubled than they had feared. Henry persuaded himself, more or less, that uncertain circumstances helped one to enjoy the passing moment, and that living in the moment was the solution — as long, of course, as the moment was bearable.

It was, admittedly, disconcerting to have staying in the house for rather a lot of moments, indeed two whole months, an old friend of theirs from Mentone, Frances Watson. She was not the only person escaping from the Riviera who descended on them but she stayed the longest and was the most demanding since she was alone and they felt a responsibility towards her. They had known her since they moved to France, a woman of their own age, widowed quite recently. She was in every way pleasant though it was difficult to remember any of her distinguishing characteristics. Now at last she had a distinguishing characteristic, though these days it was not such a rare one: she was a refugee, as she would often remark, accompanying the statement with a rueful laugh, which was not really irritating if one was ready for it. She had left Mentone in a hurry when war was declared, had come to them, as some of her kindest friends, on the train, a long and painful journey, had few possessions with her and little money, wanted to return to England but was not sure how to do it. To repay their hospitality she insisted all the time on helping, even though there was not much to help with. She became increasingly distracted, pored over railway timetables, sent telegrams to England to her sister and brother-in-law, fidgeted in a self-abnegating way. She reminded them all the time, without ever saying anything to that effect, that shelter in Pau was only temporary, that flight to England was the sensible option, that their little nest might soon be disturbed by a great black cuckoo ...

They wished after a while that she would fly away, and so she did. She left at the end of October, on a boat from Bordeaux, and though a little note arrived some time later to say she had arrived safely, she passed out of their lives.

They heard from the boys. Francis and Lucy did not wait until the following April for a stylish marriage but had a hasty wedding in a small church in Kent, the week the war broke out. The Williamsons could not go, of course, but they held many discussions over the right present to give, one of these days, in addition to the very handsome cheque they had already sent. The new-marrieds moved into the house in Chelsea. Helen thought a great deal about this house, imagining all its rooms, wondering where they would put all the things she had given Francis over the years and whether Lucy was interested in arranging rooms as she, Helen, was. She feared not: Lucy was too intellectual probably to care much. She wished she could be there to give advice. Charles had gone into the Army, into Intelligence, they gathered, since they were never told for sure. Occasionally letters arrived, assuring them that he was all right and that the Army was much less disagreeable than he had feared and that some of the people were quite congenial and interesting. But where he was, they were not told.

Christmas was difficult, in spite of the efforts Betty made on their behalf. The cook went away for a week to join her family, and Victorine travelled back to Roquebrune for a few days. Betty cooked simple but rather delicious dishes for them, and Helen helped her with the easier tasks, taking pleasure in her new role as kitchenmaid, as she described herself. She had never engaged in cooking before, or not since she had played at cooking as a child, and she was intrigued to see how ingredients changed under the influence of heat. Betty was glad to hear her laugh several times, something she had not heard for some time.

The New Year was not celebrated. There did not seem much reason to celebrate.

They had no more visitors from England.

The number of British people in Pau steadily diminished. The English Club closed. So did the English church. So did the English grocer's.

Henry bought a Luger from an English family who were returning home and were anxious to dispose of as many things they could. He showed it, with some hesitation, to Helen, and told her he had bought it to reassure her that in case of trouble they had the means to defend themselves. 'I've hardly ever seen a gun like this,' she said, taking it into her hands. He had not expected her to do this and did not care for it. But she continued to hold the Luger for a while, almost cradling it. And again she said, 'I've hardly ever seen a little gun like this.'

✦ 26 MAY 1940 ✦

Letter from Henry Williamson to Charles Williamson

Villa Hirondelle, Pau,
26 May 1940

My dear old boy

I hope that this letter will reach you by some means or another – everything that we used to rely on seems uncertain these days. We are altogether in the dark about money – we can't get any from the bank, so we are living off our envelopes full of francs which are still pretty full but not as thick as they once were. The atmosphere here in Pau is strange, not many people on the streets, hardly any of the loungers in the cafés and on the pavements who were so numerous until only a week or so ago, all gossiping about the war and bursting with absurd rumours. Occasional lorryloads of soldiers career through the town but it's not clear where they're going – they seem to disappear almost as soon as they arrive. At least they're still French soldiers rather than Germans. The newest development is the trail of refugees who once they have arrived here can't go any further unless they sneak into Spain, carloads of people with all sorts of odd possessions, mattresses and cooking pots and huge suitcases. Perhaps we shall be like them ourselves in a little while – I don't know how many suitcases and hat boxes your mother would consider appropriate in such circumstances. Some of them, I suppose the prosperous ones, book into the hotels, but many of the hotels are closing. Otherwise they set up camp in the park or drift off, I suppose into the countryside. But the good people of Pau stay at home and the Place Royale which used to be so animated is quite empty.

Most of our English acquaintances (not that there are many left here, and we never had the chance to meet many people) have gone. The ones who stay talk all the time about whether they should stay or leave. No more tea parties now, still less lunch, but a meeting in the town is quite an event. And of course we all discuss how best to leave, if we do decide to go. It's not easy, now, to know.

My dear old fellow, I don't exactly know what to tell you about us. We are trying to stay calm and rational. Not so easy always. We don't enjoy the prospect of staying here and perhaps being interned. Goodness knows what internment would mean — I don't suppose they would kill us. It's clear that our quiet life cannot continue, indeed it is already breaking up. Betty probably leaves us at the end of the month, to go back to Scotland. She thinks she can find a passage from Marseilles, though goodness knows how. Our plan is to give her Helen's jewels, so that she can hand them on to you and Francis and Lucy. Just in case we don't meet again for a while.

Actually, the atmosphere here in Pau is not at all comfortable. There are a number of odd people, quite violent-looking some of them, straying around the town. In the quarter where we are, many of the houses are closed or apparently closed, the gates locked, the shutters down.

No one seems to have broken into any of the houses around here as yet but we think it may happen quite soon since they offer so much temptation. I have bought a Luger from some of our friends who were leaving, just in case we have trouble in the night. Or even in the day, I suppose.

Your mother is being very brave. But to be honest, I don't know that she can face trying to make the journey home to England. The journey itself is bound to be painful and uncertain and dangerous, but we'd try it if we knew what it might lead to. Only we don't, any more than anyone knows anything these days. It looks, doesn't it – I hope this letter won't be censored for disloyal defeatist thoughts – as though England will be invaded? I can't see how the English can withstand the Germans, who are hideously well organised and powerful. To be honest, I don't believe that Britain has the pluck, or the strength, to fight a successful war – no morale any longer.

This present war is such a dreadful one. It leaves no one in peace. But I suppose we're lucky to have enjoyed tranquillity for so many years.

I hope you are well, dear old fellow, and wish we could see you again. It's been such a pleasure these past few years to visit you and meet your friends and see you so well and happily established, and to know your writing meets with so much approval (it certainly does from me). We're very proud of you, and we try not to worry about your safety.

I only hope that this letter reaches you. I'm writing to Francis too. I wonder if you ever see him?

Your mother sends her fondest love. She doesn't have the heart to write, just now, but she wants you to know that she thinks about all of you all the time.

Very much love from your always devoted Pa

PS I've been reading your first novel again. I think it's very sensitive and acute, and shows your fascination with people. Your mother has all the reviews – I don't think they do you justice. I would have written something much warmer!

ETTY WAS NOT GIVEN to sentimentality, and in
leaving Pau for a destination which she hoped would
ultimately prove to be Aberdeen, she showed no more leanings
towards sentimentality than ever. She prepared her luggage
with deliberation, packing only the clothes she would need for
the journey and a few garments of fine quality which in the
present circumstances she could hardly hope to replace, some
brooches and other jewellery of her own (much of which, she
realised, the Williamsons had given her), her Bible and prayer
book, and the handsome leather toilet case that was also a
present from the Williamsons. All of this she could put in one
small suitcase, which was serviceable but not so obviously
expensive that it would invite unwanted attention. She also
took a large bag. In this she placed her money (rather a lot of
it, she thought, mostly sterling, and she hoped it would be
usable); her passport (how helpful would that be? Would the
exhortations of His Britannic Majesty's Principal Secretary of
State for Foreign Affairs exert any influence on the French
police or the Spanish border guards or, worse, the German
soldiers she might have to deal with?); a little knife, useful for
oranges and extreme emergencies; and the Williamsons' jewels. She would have been happier not taking these, but then
she would have been happier if many circumstances had been
different. There was no other reliable way of taking the jewels

home to the children. She only hoped this stratagem would prove reliable – though the jewels could serve as currency at a time when elegance or self-adornment were irrelevant.

Though she had left many of her possessions at Mentone and sent a few back to Scotland a year earlier, there was still a good deal of stuff left in her room at Pau. She considered what should be done with this. Should she pack everything up and send it away, somehow? Or give it to refugees? Or put it into suitcases and leave these neatly in the attic against the day when she could collect it all? The planning and good order that had occupied so much of her life seemed completely, ludicrously, pointless. All those plans for the future and all that organisation of good order – had led her only to this chaos.

She tried not to think about her conversation with Helen a week earlier, when her old friend had made the strangest proposal to her over their future. Over the past two or three years Betty had grown used to living under a constant burden of apprehension. These days, unpleasant and frightening possibilities needed, she found, to be deposited like bags in a left-luggage office, to be called for one day. It made a great change from her childhood when she and her sister had been trained to face problems at once and to deal with them as efficiently as possible. She could not face recalling this conversation too vividly, though at the time her answer to Helen's suggestion had been decisive and almost abrupt. She had lived with the Williamsons for almost thirty years and in all those years had never known in them any anger towards her or any failing in kindness or thoughtfulness. She loved them and she loved their children, and would be loyal in any way she reasonably could be. But

Helen's proposal had made her angry, in a way she did not altogether understand.

By the time she was preparing to leave, the anger had gone. Though not given to introspection, she could not avoid, at this peculiar stage in her life, being aware of the sensations that crowded upon her. As she made her uncertain plans for departure – Marseilles seemed after all the most likely place from which she would be able to leave – she felt detached from the plans she was devising and even from the anxieties and sadness some part of her was experiencing. Sadness can wait, a voice within her would say – no time for sadness now. She was surprised to recognise in herself a certain buoyancy. It was hardly excitement, rather a reawakening of curiosity about the future, a sensation she had hardly experienced in the past years of calm routine.

This detachment remained with her on the last morning at Pau. She ate her breakfast as usual, consuming (as a first precaution) rather more than she usually did. She remarked to herself that this was the first time for many years she had breakfasted with the Williamsons without at the back of her mind having to plan for the day ahead. They had all been busy the night before with conversation and apparently happy reminiscence, but this morning words did not come easily, everything seemed either portentous or banal. So they discussed in detail the modest picnic that Victorine had prepared for Betty, and the probable unreliability of the trains, as well as the selection of books that Betty was taking for the journey.

After breakfast Betty said goodbye to Victorine, embracing her with emotion, but hardly with words or tears. She gave Victorine an envelope filled with francs – they might be useful to her, Betty thought. She was embraced by Henry who apologised again that he could not drive her to the station, the car being defunct. Helen dealt with the unbearable situation, the situation that she had for many years frequently anticipated in weighted flippancy, by flying around the hall, presenting Betty with a little unexpected packet, expressing her worries on many trivial scores before recalling herself, drawing herself up, giving her friend a single direct look and saying, 'Betty, thank you. Thank you for everything you have done for us, over all these years. We...' She did not say, 'We could not have lived without you,' although the words were felt between them.

Too true, these words seemed now, too true.

None of them wept, or if they did it was only scattered tears that could be brushed away. Time for tears later. Betty smiled instead, turned, stepped into her taxi, and was gone.

It was towards Tours that what still remained of the Government in Paris began to make its way on the evening of June 10th ... On the roads an uninterrupted procession of lorries, limousines, light cars, coaches and carts were conveying a whole people who were emigrating no one knew whither. There were some who came from the plains of Belgium, from the North, from the East, driven thence by the fighting; from Normandy, whence families who had taken refuge there at the beginning of the war, as in an inaccessible shelter, now hastened in the face of the looming menace towards they knew not yet what province; others, finally, came from the capital, from the whole Paris region, where some districts lost almost the whole of their inhabitants.

People of every kind were mingled in this throng: those whose duties or interests compelled them to leave and those who were frankly terrified by the prospect of contact with the invader: old men, women, youngsters, children, all sorts and conditions of mankind; groups of young folk who, even in misfortune, were yet determined to find amusement in the slightest incident along the road; youths ... who slipped in and out on bicycles among the strings of vehicles, laughing as they went ... and, hard by, old folk, their faces worn by anxiety, sitting on trunks or cases, carrying with them what they had been able to grasp, at random seemingly, at the moment of flight.

In the hamlets, villages and towns it was impossible to find a bit of bread; others who had gone that way already had exhausted all supplies; in certain places the inhabitants shut themselves up behind their doors as though they feared that all this crowd might requisition their mattresses! Elsewhere the line passed between two hedges of curious onlookers, who stared as if watching a procession; at times a breach opened at a cross-roads, and then the dense crowd came together again as tightly as before; progress was yard by yard...

ELIE J. BOIS, *Truth on the Tragedy of France*, 1941

✦ 26 JUNE 1940 ✦

HELEN TOOK SOME TROUBLE over the menu. The selection of foodstuffs in the shops, many of which were closed or had little for sale, was not promising, but with the cook's advice she contrived a modestly pleasant dinner. Cold leek soup, risotto, pears in brandy. They seldom ate anything heavier in the evening.

So many papers and drawers had been sorted in the previous days that there was nothing more to do of a practical nature. How should she spend that afternoon? she wondered. She took a rest after lunch, in the unexpected warmth of that early summer. As she hovered above sleep she could hear around the house the occasional sound of doors opening and closing, the noise of the radio (almost the only contact they had now with the outside world). Then distant thunder and raindrops on the lead roof of the balcony outside her window. Within her room — which was pretty, she thought, even though she had had only a year to work on it, and the dressing-table still was not right but no need to worry now, she was exhausted by worry — she felt cocooned and safe. Not that she was really safe, of course. But she would be, soon.

She looked at her Bible, which had been given to her for her confirmation. She could not at all remember the person who had dutifully inscribed it as 'her affectionate godfather'.

What on earth had happened to him? He had certainly not shown any interest in her or left her anything in his will — perhaps he was a relation of her mother and felt embarrassed. But looking at one's Bible (with which she was unfamiliar, had scarcely consulted it since childhood) seemed an appropriate thing to do at a moment like this. She stared at some pages of St John's Gospel which, she remembered from some lesson at her beastly school, was supposed to be the most spiritual one, or the most accurate, she did not quite remember. But though she read some verses she found nothing there to console her.

After a while she rose, smoothing down the blue silk counterpane with its pattern of forget-me-nots which she had brought from Lou Paradou. It looked, she noticed, less fresh than it had in the golden days. Since this was a notable day, she chose for the afternoon a white dress, one that held special memories for her. She had worn it on a number of important days in her life, and it still fitted though adjustments had had to be made by Emma. (She missed Emma for her conversation and daily care and kindness. Well, she had been fortunate, no doubt about that.) Wearing this dress at once made her feel stronger.

She went downstairs for tea. No cakes today, there were no cakes to be found in the town. But there was bread and butter, and jam. She ate some bread and butter, but did not have the stomach for jam. Henry was in a silent mood but complimented her on her appearance. She found this reassuring since she now had to attend to her own needs. The absence of a lady's maid, rather surprisingly, seemed to make life easier, allowing her to spend less time on dressing and choose more simply from her wardrobe.

Victorine was subdued. The activity in the house over the past few days indicated to her that some sort of action was being planned – indeed her employers needed to take action if they were not to be engulfed. But nothing had been said about the nature of these plans. She supposed that they were planning to flee to England by some mysterious route and could reveal no details. Anxious though she was for their sake, and a little hurt at not having been taken into their confidence, she tried to look as cheerful as usual.

During tea, she noticed, neither Monsieur nor Madame spoke. This was unusual, Mrs Williamson having been brought up to consider conversation an obligatory accompaniment to food.

After tea the Williamsons went outside. They walked round the garden, admiring the modest alterations they had made – though since their gardener had been called up the lawn was slipping back into the disorder of a year before. They stepped through the front gates into the avenue. It was very still. Even more of the houses were shuttered up than they had been two or three days before, even though they were perhaps occupied, it was hard to tell. This was a very quiet corner of the town, and probably deceptive. God knows what might be happening in the centre.

When they returned to the house, it was still only half past six. Must we wait? Helen asked herself. She looked at her husband, who understood her. He nodded. 'I think we should do everything as planned,' he said. 'Suppose I read to you?'

'Yes, Henry,' she said, 'read to me, darling. Whatever you would like.'

The Oxford Book of English Verse stood on the shelf among a handful of books they had brought with them. He read to her some of the poems they had particularly enjoyed in the past. She sat on the pink satin sofa she had always favoured, looking out through the window at the garden. It looked pretty enough from a distance. He read to her for a long time, as he had read so much and so often during their years together. Andrew Marvell he read, a poet they had always admired, and she insisted on 'Thoughts in a Garden', which would remind them, she said, of their garden in Mentone –

> How vainly men themselves amaze
> To win the palm, the oak, or bays,
> And their incessant labours see
> Crown'd from some single herb or tree,
> Whose short and narrow-verged shade
> Does prudently their toils upbraid;
> While all the flowers and trees do close
> To weave the garlands of repose

And then she asked for a poem by Yeats which they had often read, 'When you are old and grey and full of sleep...' As so often, the reading created a sense of intimacy, of a little world that belonged to them alone. He read beautifully, she thought, so intelligently, showing such sympathy for the qualities of the language.

'Being reminded of this poetry and of all the people who have created it,' he said, 'it's hard to feel wholly pessimistic. But what strikes me at such a moment – it has for a while – is that what we have now, what we are now, is all we shall ever have or be. Final. *Punkt.* It's very odd to know that there are no alternatives any more.'

He stood up and moved to the window, beside her chair but a little apart, not taking the hand which she half lifted towards him. As he looked at the neat French garden outside, he went on, 'D'you remember once, travelling in the countryside in England when we were very young, and seeing a little lane between thick hedges which overarched it? It looked strangely inviting – d'you remember? And I said that though we had no time to explore, one day we'd come back and see where the lane led.'

'I don't remember,' she said. 'Where was it?'

'Now I realise,' he said quietly, 'that we shall never go down that little lane.'

'It's better this way,' she said. 'There's no need to travel down lanes now. We're celebrating our love, my darling.'

They sat in silence until it was time for dinner. After all, there was everything to do, and there was nothing. Conversation seemed superfluous. The summer afternoon light softened but hardly changed. When Helen opened the windows on to the garden the fragrance of the drenched flowers filled their drawing room.

She thought of changing again for dinner into a black dress but Henry said, no, white had always been her best colour. But she did want the dinner table to look special. She arranged a bowl of white roses on the table, and in the sideboard Victorine found a number of wax candles, something they had not been able to buy for a while. Some had been used but a knife made them look fairly respectable. The silver candlesticks they had brought from home were placed on the sideboard and the dining table.

As Helen lit the candles before dinner, she felt that she was partaking in some ancient ceremony, rather as she might have felt as a young girl. She was reminded of the evenings of her youth at Blithbury, lighting the candles at dinner for her aunt and her father. How strange it was, she reflected, that within this grown person, within this ageing body, still flowered the spirit of youth. Inside me, she thought, still lives that young and eager Helen who would open the French windows at Blithbury in the dawn and run across the grass to the Chinese bridge.

Lighting the candles, arranging the silver bowl of roses on the table, placing the napkins (twisted by Victorine with her usual skill into spirals) on the plates, she could forget what was happening. She had always been a good hostess, she knew — and this faculty had not deserted her. She felt strong, knowing that everything was accomplished that could be, and that her dear husband was at her side.

'*Madame est servie*,' said Victorine, as she had said before so many lunches and on so many evenings, though now she usually only appeared at the door of the room and smiled. Dear Victorine, their friend for so many years.

At dinner they ate little, only enough to give the impression of normality. Even in these times of chaos and fear, Helen felt, dignity must be preserved in outward forms, embodying the civilised ideals in which they had been raised. Dressed in white as she was, with Henry so distinguished in his dark grey suit, did they not resemble a couple at their wedding breakfast?

They had coffee at table. It was not very good. There was no decent coffee left in the house, and it was hard to find any more in the shops. No matter.

When Victorine had served the coffee, Henry said to her, '*Ça sera tout, Victorine. Nous vous remercions pour tout ce que vous avez fait pour nous.'* And as she looked at him, consideringly, he continued, *'Adieu, Victorine.'*

'Adieu' – how strange the word, how strange to hear it spoken, as it so seldom was. Helen rose, and pressed Victorine's hands between hers. The maid was startled – but then, however long she had known them, and however fond of them she might be, they were still in some ways strangers to her. What these words might mean she did not know.

When she had gone, they sat in silence for a while. It was dusk and outside there was no sound at all.

'This must be the moment, Helen. Let us say goodbye.'

'Not goodbye, my darling,' she answered. 'We are together now, as we've always been. As we shall always be.'

'Yes, we are together,' said Henry. 'You're the most important person to me in the world, Helen. We've been so happy together, haven't we?'

'Lovey darling . . .' she said. Only that.

They went into the drawing room. They embraced. Henry unlocked the drawer of the writing table, and took out the large Luger, which she had only once seen. She touched it tentatively, with one finger. They did not say any more.

He did not need to check the gun. He knew it was loaded.

She sat on her little satin sofa, with her hands folded across her breast. She smiled at him for one last time. He shot her in the head. She fell on to the ground, in a heap of white muslin.

When he saw that she was dead, he thought of nothing except the actions that he must take next. He was, he supposed, technically a murderer. But that did not matter except in the legal sense, since they were partners in a pact. He closed her eyes and covered her body with a rug he had prepared for the purpose.

Henry did not want to cause more trouble to Victorine and whoever would have to take them away than he had to. He hoped that he could do what he had to do, cleanly. He knelt beside the body of his wife, then raised the gun to his head, and shot himself.

He had left a short note for Victorine on the table, explaining what they had done. And as much money as he still had.

A FINAL LETTER from the Williamsons to their sons did arrive in England, via a friend of theirs who at the last minute escaped from France via Spain and Portugal. It took several weeks to reach its destination, weeks when the sons had no idea of their parents' fate. One evening Francis had a telephone call from this friend, telling him that he had left the Williamsons in good health but knew nothing of their plans, and saying that there was a letter on its way.

The letter arrived the next day. Their father told them that they had decided to take their own lives. Helen could not face the attempt to escape. France was in chaos. England provided no sort of refuge that they could trust. To flee to Canada and start a completely new life with their Canadian cousins was more than she could manage.

For my own part [wrote Henry] I would try the experiment since life still seems to me worth investigating and I can't help being interested in what happens to the society we have known all our lives. But your mother does not have the strength to face the unknown, and life here is becoming so uncomfortable and difficult. She's terrified that we might be taken away, and perhaps separated from one another. She wants us to end our lives, and I still love her enough to do as she wants.

Our greatest hope is that you will survive, and that England will remain a tolerable place for all of you to live in. You know how much we love you, and how happy you have made us, each in your own way. We are very proud of you. I'm afraid that the decision we've made will upset you. Above all, you're not to feel guilty — there's no need. We've created our own death, just as we created our own lives.

If our bodies are ever returned to you — which seems extremely unlikely — I want them to be buried very plainly, no headstone if possible, certainly no inscription about us. Everything to be as simple as possible — that's what's appropriate.

God bless you all, dearest children . . .

⤚⇒ AUTHOR'S FOOTNOTE ⇐⤙

This book is inspired by the lives of my grandparents,
who lived at Menton from 1913 to 1939. The house in
the story is based on their house (which survives), and many
of the details of the leading characters' way of life derive
from information I have been able to gather about them.
The dialogue and many of the events are drawn from
my own imaginings. In depicting the sons I have
interpreted my father's and uncle's
lives very freely.

This book is not intended as a memoir, nor as a tribute.
I never knew the people from whom the principal
characters are drawn, and feel detached from them.
But theirs is a story which has always interested and
saddened me. I felt that, refracted through the
form of fiction, it deserved to be told.

JENNIFER JOHNSTON

Two Moons

In a house overlooking Dublin Bay, Mimi and her daughter Grace are disturbed by the unexpected arrival of Grace's daughter Polly and her striking new boyfriend. The events of the next few days will move both of them to reassess the shape of their lives. For while Grace's visitors lead her to consider an uncertain future, Mimi, who receives a messenger of a very different kind, must begin to set herself to rights with the betrayals and disappointments of the past.

'Superbly executed . . . both enchanted and enchanting' *Daily Telegraph*

'A marvellously affirmative and exhilarating novel which satisfies like a gorgeous piece of music. More please' Clare Boylan, *Image Magazine*

'Mesmerising . . . a richly atmospheric coupling of fairy-tale conceit and raw emotional urgency' *Daily Express*

0 7472 5932 1

review

RONAN BENNETT

The Catastrophist

Shortlisted for the 1998 Whitbread Novel Award.

Gillespie, an Irishman, goes to the Congo in pursuit of his beautiful Italian lover Inès. Unlike her, Gillespie has no interest in the story of the deepening independence crisis, nor in the charismatic leader, Patrice Lumumba. He has other business: this is his last chance for love.

'Bennett's writing is as lush and sensual as ripe mangos . . . The tone, which is perfectly pitched, and the exotic setting collude to evoke an era of colonial decadence' *Financial Times*

'Glowing with psychological insight . . . I have not read such a good thriller in years . . . The prose is as sharp as a whip, though subtle and poetic' Ian Thomson, *Evening Standard*

'A great achievement, an impressive testament to the appeal of strong narrative and sympathetic characterisation' *Sunday Telegraph*

'A memorable book, with a ring of deeply felt authenticity' Hugo Hamilton, *Sunday Tribune*

0 7472 6033 8

review

SANDRA GULLAND

The Many Lives & Secret Sorrows of Joséphine B.

You will be unhappily wed. You will be widowed. You will be Queen.

To the fourteen-year-old Rose, eldest daughter of a poor plantation landlord, the fortuneteller's prophecy is both thrilling and laughable. Poorly educated and without a dowry, it seems unlikely that she will find any husband – much less a king. But history tells a different tale, for Rose not only marries into a wealthy aristocratic family, she survives the French Revolution, outlives her first husband and is one day known as Joséphine Bonaparte.

In this beautifully crafted novel, Sandra Gulland pulls back the veil of history to reveal an extraordinary life. From her simple childhood on the French island of Martinique to her first heady experience in French revolutionary Paris and her unhappy marriage to the unfaithful Alexandre, Rose's destiny lives with a man determined to rule all of France, determined to make her Queen.

This is the first book in an incredible trilogy inspired by the life of Joséphine Bonaparte.

'By casting her narrative in the form of a first-person journal, Gulland invests it with vividness and immediacy, so that one sometimes forgets it is a historical novel, and reads it with a real sense of surprise at each development' *Times Metro*

0 7472 6189 X

review

SARA GEORGE

The Journal of Mrs Pepys
Portrait of a Marriage

The highly acclaimed, bestselling fictional journal of the wife of our most celebrated diarist.

'An altogether enchanting novel . . . sheds a brilliant beam into the dark interior of this 17th-century household and with compassion elegantly scripts a couple's most intimate moments' *Scotland on Sunday*

'Sara George has succeeded admirably in finding a voice – and a sweet, innocent but intelligent and warm voice it is – for one of the many women half-hidden from history by their dominant menfolk' Margaret Foster

'Pepys's wife finds her voice . . . all the more powerful for being partial' *Daily Telegraph*

'Anyone who thinks that Bridget Jones epitomises an existence turbulent with trials and tribulations should take a look at Elizabeth Pepys's journal . . . The minutiae of daily life against the huge events of fire and plague echo Pepys but in a far more accessible form; Elizabeth is an attractive creation and this piece of "faction" makes a spirited tale' *Independent on Sunday*

0 7472 5761 2

review

If you enjoyed this book here is a selection of other bestselling titles from Review